Brief Loves That Live Forever

Also by Andreï Makine

Brief Loves
That
Live Forever

╫· ╫· ╫· *A Novel*

Andreï Makine

Translated from the French by Geoffrey Strachan

GRAYWOLF PRESS

This publication is made possible, in part, by the voters of Minnesota through a Minnesota State Arts Board Operating Support grant, thanks to a legislative appropriation from the arts and cultural heritage fund, and through a grant from the Wells Fargo Foundation Minnesota. Significant support has also been provided by Target, the McKnight Foundation, Amazon.com, and other generous contributions from foundations, corporations, and individuals. To these organizations and individuals we offer our heartfelt thanks.

Published by Graywolf Press
250 Third Avenue North, Suite 600
Minneapolis, Minnesota 55401

www.graywolfpress.org

Published in the United States of America

ISBN 978-1-55597-712-2

2 4 6 8 9 7 5 3 1
First Graywolf Printing, 2015

Library of Congress Control Number: 2014960049

Cover design: Kyle G. Hunter

Cover art: istockphoto.com

To the memory of Dick Seaver

Translator's Note

Andreï Makine was born and brought up in Russia, but *Brief Loves That Live Forever*, like his other novels, was written in French. The book is set mainly in Russia, but also in France, and the author uses some Russian words in the French text that I have retained in this English translation. These include *shapka* (a fur hat or cap, often with earflaps), *izba* (a traditional wooden house built of logs), *kolkhoz* (a collective farm in the former Soviet Union), *Komsomol* (the Soviet Communist League of Youth), *apparatchik* (a member of the Soviet Communist Party administration, or *apparat*), *nomenklatura* (the public positions filled by Party appointees), *gulag* (the system of Soviet corrective labor camps), and *samizdat* (the clandestine publication of texts banned in the Soviet Union and also the texts themselves).

Other Russian historical references include the famous Nevsky Prospekt, one of the main streets in St. Petersburg (formerly Leningrad), and "Potemkin villages," sham villages reputedly built for Catherine the Great's tour of the Crimea in 1787 on the orders of her chief minister, Potemkin. The writer Varlam Shalamov was in the Kolyma gulag in the far north of the Soviet Union from 1937 to 1951. His stories of life there were published in English as *Kolyma Tales*. As a result of calendar

changes, the date when the October Revolution was celebrated throughout the Soviet Union was November 7. "Shock workers" were members
of "shock brigades," bodies of (especially voluntary) workers who took on
particularly arduous tasks.

I am indebted to many people, including the author, for advice, assistance,
and encouragement in the preparation of this translation. To all of them
my thanks are due, notably: Thompson Bradley, Mary Byers, Ludmilla
Checkley, June Elks, Geoffrey Ellis, Julian Evans, Mary Rose Goodwin,
Scott Grant, Martyn Haxworth, Andrew Lawson, Catherine Merridale,
Pierre Sciama, Simon Strachan, Susan Strachan, and Roger Wilmut, as
well as my editor at Graywolf Press, Katie Dublinski.

GS

Brief Loves That Live Forever

ONE

The Tiny Minority

From my youth onward the memory of that chance encounter returns, at once insistent and elusive, like a riddle one never gives up hope of solving.

These are the facts. One day in spring I am walking home with a friend, a man in poor health. Suddenly he proposes that we go through the center of the city, lengthening our journey by a diversion that is especially puzzling, since he can have no love for this city in northern Russia, where every street reminds him of his tormented life. He stops close to a park fence, overcome by a fit of coughing, and turns aside, one hand clamped over his mouth, the other gripping an iron railing. At this very moment a woman steps out of a car a few yards away from where we have halted. She is holding the hand of a little boy, who glances at us with alarmed curiosity. In his eyes we look like a couple of drunkards about to throw up. The unease I feel does not banish a vaguer notion, more difficult to pinpoint in my mind. Obscurely I sense that our detour was not a matter of chance, nor was the appearance of this beautiful stranger . . . She walks past, leaving us with a swift tremor of perfume, bitter and chill, and at once the entrance opens to one of the apartment buildings that surround the park, and the caretaker admits the woman and child. My friend straightens up, we continue on our way. This chance encounter—its fleeting strangeness—leaves its mark on me at the time and returns throughout my life, long remaining an unsolved mystery.

There must be barely half a dozen people in the world today who remember Dmitri Ress. In my own memory just two very ill-matched fragments are preserved. Two pieces from a mosaic, which, if one did not know Ress, might be thought unconnected.

The first, this ruefully clumsy remark made by someone who knew him well: "He loved her . . . in a way one cannot be loved . . . other than far away from this earth."

The second fragment—his activity as a dissident—was generally spoken of with the same puzzled hesitation. This was not a case of indifference toward a forgotten hero on the part of those who survived him. It was more a simple inability to grasp the logic underlying the struggle Ress waged until his death. For some, a quixotic battle, for others an act of suicide that continued over twenty years.

When first I met him, at the age of forty-four, bald, toothless, and ravaged by cancer, he looked like a sickly octogenarian. Taken together, his three successive criminal convictions amounted to a total of fifteen years and some few months spent behind barbed wire. The harshness of the sentences related to the originality of his beliefs: a philosopher by training, he criticized not the specific defects of the regime that held sway in the Russia of those days but the servility with which all men in all ages renounce intelligence to follow the herd.

"But why, in that case, do you direct your fury against our country?" he would be asked under interrogation. "Because it's my native land," he would reply. "And I find it particularly intolerable to see my compatriots dozing around a hog wallow."

The upholders of the law perceived this as subversiveness of the worst kind. They preferred dealing with "classic" dissidents, who allowed themselves to be deported to the West, where the sharpest of pens were quickly blunted by well-sated indifference.

It was at the age of twenty-two that Dmitri Ress committed his first offense. On the eve of the traditional parade to mark the anniversary of the October Revolution, he put up a poster on the wall of an administrative building, executed with a real draftsman's talent: the grandstand to which the Party dignitaries ascended, the sea of red flags, the banners covered in slogans glorifying communism, the two lines of soldiers forming a conduit for the forward progress of the patriotic demonstrators. Totally realistic. Except that the notables standing upright on the platform, the solid silhouettes topped off with soft felt hats, were shown as pigs. Little contemptuous eyes, snouts bloated with fat. And as the "popular masses" reached the foot of the grandstand they, too, were undergoing the start of this metamorphosis. The poster was captioned "Long Live the Great October Pork Harvest!"

This was a serious offense, but its perpetrator's youth might have inspired clemency. All the more so because his zoological conceit was not new, all dissident literature made use of such devices, Solzhenitsyn himself compared one of the members of the nomenklatura to a brutal and lecherous boar. It would have been possible to plead a foolish error, the malign influence of things he had read . . . Unfortunately the young man proved to be arrogant, claiming he had painted what he saw, determined to denounce the whole animal pack. An indefensible attitude.

Nevertheless the judges showed some indulgence: three years in an ordinary penal colony.

Instead of making him compliant, the camp made him stubborn. As soon as he was released, he offended again. Drawings and pamphlets that now fell into a more grievous category: anti-Soviet propaganda. In short, he made matters worse for himself. Which caused a judge, exasperated by so much inflexibility, to resort to a Russian expression that means, more or less, "Never crawl into the neck of a bottle."

If only he had followed the logic of those dissidents who sounded off against the Kremlin and idolized the West. But no, he stuck to his guns: his graphic and literary output targeted the whole of humanity and his native land was merely one instance among others. He took a five-year sentence in his stride. Another, the last, in a camp "with a strict regime," broke him physically but confirmed the flinty solidity of his convictions. What is more, he looked like a long shard of flint and on occasion his eyes flashed with glints of fire, flying sparks from an unconquered mind in a broken body.

All I learned about that bruised life was limited to this tally of three convictions and a few rare details of his daily life as prisoner . . . And also the nickname "Poet," which his fellow prisoners had given him, though I did not know if its implication was disparaging or approving. That was all. Ress made it a point of honor not to talk about his sufferings.

The only long conversation we had took place in a city in northern Russia six hundred miles from Moscow, the place of residence assigned to him during the last six months of his life.

It was May Day. I was walking home with him and we had to wait for a while at the entrance to a bridge, closed off on account of the parade taking place on the main square. Leaning on the rail, we could see the procession advancing past an immense building, the local Party headquarters. On the grandstand's terraces stood rows of black overcoats and felt hats.

The day was sunny but icy and windy. Bursts of military marches were borne on the breeze, snatches of slogans flung out by the loudspeakers, the dull roar from the columns of participants as they repeated these official watchwords at the tops of their voices.

"Just picture it! The very same spectacle all the way from the Far East to the Polish frontier," Ress murmured, in the dreamy tones one adopts when conjuring up a fabled land. "And from the Arctic Ocean to the deserts of central Asia. The same grandstands, the same pigs in felt hats, the same crowd stupefied by this charade. The same parade stretching for thousands and thousands of miles . . ."

The notion was striking, I had never thought about this human tide, sweeping in relays from one time zone to the next (eleven in all!) across the vast territory of the country. Yes, in every town, in every latitude, the same collectivist religious celebration.

Sensing my perplexity, he hastened to add, "And, believe me, it's the same in the camps! The top-ranking camp guards lined up on a platform, a band made up of musical ex-convicts, red banners: 'Glory,' 'Long Live,' 'Forward!' Everywhere, I tell you. One day they'll fly those grandstands up to the moon . . ."

Echoing his words, a gust of wind spat out, "Long live the heroic vanguard of the working class! . . ." Ress gave a tight-lipped smile over a toothless mouth.

"Oh those grandstands! . . . In the West they've written critical commentaries by the ton to explain this society of ours, the hierarchy, the mental enslavement undergone by the populace . . . And they still don't get it! While if you're here, all you have to do is open your eyes. You can see the chief apparatchik from here, at the center of the platform, a black hat and that face, flat as a pancake. Around him, with meticulous concern for the ranking order, his henchmen. The farther they are from him, the less important they are. Logical. The supreme example is the official platform in Red Square. A few soldiers, so the people know what power upholds the Party's authority. And most interesting of all: the enclosures that divide the platform into sectors. In the one on the right are the heads of state enterprises, the river port administration, a few high-ranking trade unionists, and, lest the proletarians be forgotten, three or four shock workers. In a nutshell, the cream of the forces of production. And as for the less productive forces, but ones still useful to the regime, they put them on the left. Heads of universities, editors of local newspapers, bigwigs from the world of medicine, a couple of scribblers, in a word, the intelligentsia. And immediately beneath the central podium, the family enclosure where the wives and children are deposited . . ."

He was overcome by a fit of coughing, leaned forward, and a thick blue vein swelled on his temple, very prominent beneath the transparent skin of his cranium. I sought to steer the conversation in another direction.

"Fine. But, you know, the people don't really care about those grandstands . . ."

He stood up straight and his eyes burned into me.

"Wrong! The people do care about them. They need them! This pyramid of pigs' heads is essential to them as the coherent expression of the world's architecture. The way the enclosures are arranged reassures them. It's their lay religion. And that idiot bellowing slogans into the loudspeaker is the precise equivalent of a priest preaching his sermon . . ."

He managed to hold in check another coughing fit, his neck trembled, his face turned purple. His voice came out in bursts, wary of the spasms clutching at his throat.

"We shouldn't generalize . . . They're not all the same . . . these demonstrators. You could say there are . . . three groups. The first, the overwhelming majority, are a docile mass who like the comfort of the herd. The second category is made up of cynics, mainly from the intelligentsia: they chorus the slogans, but when they chant it's all a game, it's a joke. They wave their flags in ironic frenzy. They brandish the leaders' portraits on their poles as if they were heads held aloft on pikes. The third and last category is that of the rebels, naive enough to hope they can disrupt this grotesque parade. They write pamphlets, make posters, and . . . and . . ."

He began coughing again, one hand covering his mouth, the other seizing the parapet of the bridge. His thin body's bent shape, clad in an old raincoat, was reminiscent of a broken branch . . . The path had just been reopened, the parade was coming to an end, the crowd could be seen dispersing into the neighboring streets.

We continued our walk, but instead of going toward his home,

Ress led me into a residential quarter of the Stalin era: a park surrounded by a rectangle of apartment buildings where lived the notables we had just seen on the grandstand. He stopped beside the cast-iron fence to catch his breath, watching the demonstrators on their way home, glad to be finished with the chore of compulsory participation. A young man carrying the portrait of a member of the Politburo over his shoulder. Three adolescent girls, each with a rolled-up banner tucked under her arm. A group of schoolboys . . .

And suddenly, stepping out of a black official car, an attractive woman in her forties, dressed in a pale coat, holding a little boy's hand. The child stared at us in astonishment, the presence of these two men, so unalike, must have appeared strange to him. The mother tugged at his hand, and they passed within a few yards of us before going into one of the "Stalinesque" apartment buildings. I caught a trace of perfume, subtly bitter, in harmony with that cool, luminous day. Ress turned away, coughing again, but without choking. For a moment it even seemed as if he were trying to spare the child the spectacle of his discomfort . . .

We set off again without my understanding why he had wanted to go via the park. Perhaps, simply, so as to emerge onto the main square, now almost empty . . . He nodded his head slightly in the direction of the grandstand. His voice now had a joyful ring.

"A science fiction scenario. Tomorrow this rotten regime falls apart. We find ourselves in the capitalist paradise and the people who step up onto this grandstand are millionaires, film stars, suntanned politicians . . . And in the intellectuals' enclosure, let's say, Jean-Paul Sartre . . . No, he's just died. Well, they'll find someone. And do you know what the funniest part of it is? The crowd will parade past just the same. You see, they don't care who fills the grandstand. What matters is for it to be filled. That's what gives meaning to the lives of our human ant heap. Yes, instead of the statue of Lenin, you'd have to picture a playboy in a tuxedo. It'll happen one day. And once again there'll be those three categories in the parade: placid sleepwalkers, very much in the majority, some cynics, and a few marginal rebels . . ."

He was already coughing a little as he spoke, but the real onslaught came as we began walking again. Barking and choking, which gave him the pitiful appearance of an old dog emptying its lungs of the last of its rages. I stood there helplessly, not knowing how to come to his aid, nor what to say, embarrassed and ashamed, as one always is when confronted by a person taken ill out in the street.

We had stopped on a badly paved slope, flanked by old wooden houses. At the bottom of the incline, beyond the luminous tracery of willow groves, the river could be seen glittering. Slabs of ice still clung to the banks. From time to time a cloud hid the sun and then the landscape was reminiscent of the start of winter . . .

For a moment Ress managed to control his coughing, raised his head, and, with what looked to me like a blind stare, took in the slope, the riverbank, the willows. His words came in feverish gasps.

"Yes, they'll always . . . be there . . . those three categories . . . dozing swine . . . cynics . . . and sourpusses with ruined lungs . . . like me . . ."

The cough started again and suddenly the hand he pressed to his lips was filled with red. With clumsy urgency he took out a handkerchief and I saw the fabric was already spotted with blood. A fresh spasm in his chest caused a dark clot to erupt from his mouth, then another. I hastened to offer him my handkerchief . . .

A telling detail: that silk square had been given to me by a girl-friend. Such a gift would seem incongruous today, but was evidently not unusual in the Russia of those years, and this brings home to me the almost cosmic gap that separates us from that period. But that day, as I watched Ress wiping his lips, it was the man's own past that I was speculating on: "He's not had many chances to be loved . . ." Long spells of hard labor, the painful slowness with which a prisoner's life is then rebuilt, and already another arrest, and very soon health too ravaged for any hope of a new lease on life, born of some fresh encounter, a new dream, a love affair.

He was still bent double, overcome by the lashing of the cough, the handkerchief crushed against his mouth. With the ugly stance of a drunkard overcome by nausea. Disconcerted, I would from time to time stammer a useless reassurance: "It'll calm down soon . . . You just need a glass of cold water . . ." With an intensity I had never before experienced, I sensed the atrocious injustice of life, or History, or perhaps God, at all events the cruelty of this world's indifference toward a man spitting out his blood into a silk handkerchief. A man who had never had the time to be in love.

Half the sky was already laden with clouds. A scattering of snow-flakes began to float over the rooftops, weaving a swirl of white at the end of the street. In the far distance beyond the river, the light remained daz-zling, springlike, as if that morning's motley parade were continuing over there, leaving us all alone in this little sloping street. The snow, this last snow of the year, brought with it alleviation, a fresh, deeper perspective, the silent harmony of all we could see. This silence also came from Ress getting his breath back at last, a rhythm of short, ever calmer exhalations.

His voice, freed now from the urge to argue or convince, sounded like an echo coming from a time when all he was saying would seem obvious.

"Three categories . . . The conciliators, the cynics, the rebels . . . But there are . . . There are also those who have the wisdom to pause in an alleyway like this and watch the snow falling. Notice a lamp being lit in a window. Inhale the scent of burning wood. This wisdom, only a tiny minority among us know how to live by it. In my case, I've found it too late. I'm only just getting to know it. Often, out of habit, I go back to playing the old roles. I did it just now, when I was making fun of those poor wretches on their platform. They're blind. They'll die having never seen this beauty."

What we could see was humble, gray, very poor. Houses from the previous century, their roofs bristling with dead stalks here and there. The dull air was reminiscent of dusk in November, on the brink of win-ter. We were in May, the whole city was busy with preparations for the festive meal, and the sun's brutal gaiety would return. But the beauty was there in this moment adrift between seasons. All it took was these pale colors, the untimely chill of the snow, the poignant memory of so many past winters suddenly awakened. This beauty merged into our breathing, all we had to do was to forget who we thought we were.

I do not know the precise circumstances of Ress's death, whether there was any friendly, or at least solicitous, presence with him at the end. I have my own excuses, which are the best I can come up with: travel, work, and the difficulty of remaining in contact with someone who, like him, did not even have a telephone. Besides, we had never really been close; he was "a friend of a friend of a friend."

Today, more than a quarter of a century later, as I try to remember Ress and try, as we all do from time to time in addressing people now departed or dead, to embark on a conversation where his voice might join me, what returns to me is a scattered sequence of days, from long before he and I ever met, days going back to my childhood, to my youth. They come to life again in my memory, thanks to Ress's words spoken then, his lips still stained with blood. Strangely enough, it is these glimpses of the past that offer the best response to his tortured tones. Perhaps because they were moments of tenderness lived through long, long ago, moments of love such as he himself had no time for in his life.

In these words, now silently addressed to Ress, what matters to me is letting him know he was right. We are all capable of stepping aside from the sheep-like procession of parades, with their fanatical chanting, their crushing emblems, their lies.

What matters is contriving to say this without betraying the broken voice of that man who, in one of the camps, was given the nickname of "Poet."

TWO

She Set Me Free from Symbols

She was not the first woman to have dazzled me with her beauty, with
the patient strength of her love. She was, however, the first to reveal to
me that a woman with love in her heart no longer belongs to our world
but from it creates another one where she dwells, sovereign, untouched
by the restless greed of everyday life. Yes, an extraterrestrial.

And to think that our encounter took place upon a stage set de-
vised to represent a life devoid of love!

The symbols used by officialdom are designed to affect our mental
state. When we take part in a mass spectacle, each modest self gains
the strength of ten, our voices ring out, amplified by the anthems and the
brass bands' din, the long view of History helps our fear of death to fade.
In the trompe l'oeil of propaganda each emblem conjures up a road to
be followed, a meaning to life, a future. Yes, existential tranquilizers, meta-
physical antidepressants.

As a child I was not remotely aware of this, and yet these addictive
symbols were already having their effect on me. They camouflaged the
deprivation we lived in, which would be hard to describe today, amid a
plethora of convenient, disposable objects. The world I and my comrades

saw was transparent with poverty: an iron bed in a dormitory, clothes
that, as we grew out of them, were passed on to our juniors, a single pair
of shoes, too hot in summer, too thin during the cold weather, which,
in those regions of the middle Volga, persisted bitterly right into April.
One pen (to be precise, a little rod with a nib holder at the tip of it), a few
notebooks, no books other than those we borrowed from the library, no
money, no personal possessions, no means of communicating with the
outside world.

The exuberance that filled us seemed illogical, almost uncanny.
But the only yardstick we measure happiness by is our own lives, whether
rich or destitute. After the midday meal we were entitled to a cup of hot
liquid in which a few slices of dried fruit were macerating. Having the
good luck to come upon a fig would transform one of our number into a
"chosen one"; he would relish it, closing his eyes and concentrating completely on the indescribable taste that opened up inside his mouth. We
would watch him dumbly, transported to the distant lands where such
fruits ripened . . . Much later, in a book by Solzhenitsyn, I would come
across a character in a gulag who was thrilled to trawl a tiny scrap of fish
out of his bowl of soup when the ladle chanced to scrape the bottom of
a pot. One day, talking to one of the countless prisoners from the Stalin
era, I would learn that happiness could be based on even less: a grain left
unmilled in a slice of bread . . .

Alongside these poor people's pleasures an infinitely richer happiness
was available to us, that of things imagined. We possessed so little,
and for such a short time, that the whole world was there for us to
dream about. That dazzlingly white city, for instance. I can still see
its streets bathed in sunlight, its tall, serene inhabitants walking along
unhurriedly, entering a store crammed with an abundance of things to
eat: one of them selects a bottle of lemonade, another a chocolate bar
(just one and yet there are thousands!), and they go on their way without having to pay anything . . . In answer to our questions about the
nature of communism our teacher gave us this explanation: "Money

will no longer exist. Everyone will be able to take what is sufficient for his needs . . ."

An incredulous murmur ran around the class in response to the vision we had just glimpsed: jubilant hordes storming the shops and running off laden with masses of cakes, chocolates, and ice cream . . . The teacher must have guessed at the looting we had in mind and hastened to complete her interpretation of the future: "The people who live in communist society will have a different type of conscience from ours. The shops will be full and everything will be free, but people will take only what they need. If you can return next day, why hoard?"

That scene occurred at the start of the sixties. The Party had just proclaimed that communism would arrive within the marvelously brief span of twenty years.

The idea of a new type of conscience struck my child's mind like a flash of inspiration. Yes, a shining city, smiling, fraternal people, who, amid an abundance of desirable goods and food, do not lose their heads, choose the minimum, enough to feed themselves and devote themselves to a mysterious activity referred to by our teacher as "the edification of the future." Such a task made ridiculous the desire to stuff oneself, thrusting one's neighbor aside to grab the choicest piece . . . Childhood images do not fade or vanish. That shining city has often seemed more real to me than those where I lived.

Official propaganda congealed these dream visions together into tangible, simplified language, common to the country's whole population. The two great parades of the year, for May Day and the October Revolution, gave substance to the symbolic, ideas were embodied in columns of workers, on Red Square the word was made tanks and rockets, History spoke with the voice of an endless crowd, processing from Moscow to the humblest township, past grandstands on which the leaders stood, saluting this dress rehearsal for the messianic society.

At the time I was incapable of understanding it, as I marched beside my comrades in the ranks, carrying a flag or a portrait of one of the

Party leaders. Now what remains is the memory of a mesmerized sense of belonging to this human mass, dazzlement at the sea of red banners, a state of euphoria, ecstasy even, yes, some kind of trance. But I was too young then to perceive it like that, I simply felt happy.

The May Day ceremonies have ended up merging in my memory into a single celebration, resonant with loudspeaker slogans and prolonged cheering, spattered with sprays of sunlight and scarlet flags flapping in the wind.

The autumn parades, on the other hand, have left me with quite a different recollection, an upsetting sensation for a child who truly believed in this spectacle and suddenly felt himself duped by it. That was it, the feeling of a lie guessed at behind the mise en scène.

And yet the mise en scène for that parade, politically more important than May Day, was always impeccable. The strict hierarchy governing the placing of the leaders on the grandstand, the banners proclaiming the imminence of the radiant future or lambasting American imperialism. The nimble tread of those in the parade, grouped according to their professional affiliations, the impressive steadiness of the soldiers in the honor guard, a living bulwark against the enemies of socialism. As for the symbolism, every detail was respected: the people were advancing toward that white city of the future of which I had always dreamed.

And perhaps it took no more than a fine shower of icy rain to transform the meaning of the procession that day. A purely physical discomfort, that was it, irritating to the occupants of the grandstand.

The pupils from our orphanage came right at the end of the parade, given the lack of ideological weight represented by our soberly attired ranks, our close-cropped heads, with the pale, bony faces of poorly nourished children. Just as we reached the foot of the grandstand the apparatchiks abandoned their parade ground immobility, bestirred themselves, and, in emulation of the first among them, began to move off the grandstand, exchanging discreet remarks out of the corners of their mouths. The cheering rumbled on, far too loud for us to be able to hear any of this chat, but the drift of it was clear: the dismal weather, the cold, and the delights of a copious lunch that awaited them.

Without realizing it, I had seen the wrong side of the scenery, a stage from which those sinister actors were making their exit. The grandstand was emptying, losing its symbolic significance. Heady euphoria gave way to worrying surmise, doubts I quickly stifled beneath my comrades' vociferous chanting and the smell of the red paint on rain-soaked banners . . . And yet that momentary "What's the point?" had left its mark on my naive faith.

Two days later a hallucinatory nocturnal vision reinforced my disillusionment . . . We were often sent to work in big factories on the outskirts of the city, to prepare us for manual labor, which was the lot our condition destined us for. We cleaned workshops, raked yards strewn with scrap metal, picked up waste steel or timber. That evening the truck due to take us back to the orphanage broke down and we waited until late into the night, gathered together in a warehouse . . . As we were driving back through the city a distressing spectacle confronted those who, like me, were sitting at the back of the van: there on the central square, beneath spotlight beams, workers were dismantling the grandstand! I just had time to see long sections of the terraces and a stack of portraits piled on top of one another, at random . . .

The shock was as great as if in the middle of the screening of a film I had caught sight of technicians rearranging the furniture or even tickling one of the actresses. The blatant nature of what I saw blinded me: this dismantling was done at night to conceal from the people the fact that it was all no more than scenery, a painted facade, behind which there was nothing. And yet there was something: the asphalt littered with cigarette ends, the sad sleepiness of windows in ugly houses, the bare, shivering trees. The workmen's gestures spoke of ill-tempered abruptness, weary disgust . . . The following day the square resumed its ordinary appearance, merely leaving me with a nagging thought: "That whole grandstand, they must hide it in a secret place."

An even more astounding discovery occurred at the end of the winter: the place was not secret at all!

One afternoon in February they sent us to clear the pathways in a huge park at the edge of the city, and it was there, in an area few people visited, that we came upon the parade grandstand. Nobody had thought of covering it up, except that it was blanketed in thick snow, intensely blue in the sunlight, marked by no human footprint . . .

The real mystery, however, lay not upon the snow-covered terraces but in the grandstand's entrails, a dark space, pierced through with steel poles, into which I slithered, following three or four of my comrades. The others, their shovels on their shoulders, were already lining up in ranks to return to the orphanage, just as we embarked on a long exploration of this metallic maze.

For me the adventure had a rather sacrilegious appeal: crouched beneath the terraces that were generally occupied by the Party leaders, I had just gained access to the holy of holies of power, the ladder of fame, at the very heart of a symbol! From below, I identified the place where the chief apparatchik stood, then the enclosure for the intelligentsia . . .

My reverie was shattered by a shout from outside. My comrades were calling me and their voices were vibrant with baleful glee masquerading as friendly concern. "Hey, come on! Get out of there! It's time to go back. The supervisor's going to be fuming again . . ."

Wriggling between two steel poles, I had to climb over a waist-high barrier of beams, slip with more difficulty between the next poles, crouch to pass under a fresh crossbar.

And suddenly I realized that, although this maze was of open scaffolding, there was no way out of it!

My panic was met by wild guffaws. My comrades were helpless with laughter, pointing at me as if I were a caged animal. Perfidious reassurance was added to their mockery: "Don't worry. You've got lots of time till tomorrow. Night night! Sleep well! We'll tell the supervisor you decided to bed down under the grandstand, ha, ha, ha . . ."

And they were already moving off, almost forgetting me. I knew this mixture of hardness and indifference, it was the very stuff of our young lives.

Fear robbed me of all judgment. Like a puppet on strings, I bounded about, making the same moves over and over again amid countless metal poles—crouching, swiveling, sliding, skirting . . . Reaching the last line of poles, I realized they were closer together than the preceding ones and left me no chance of escape! I also became aware that I had instinctively chosen a route that led toward the sunlight and it was the wrong route.

But all routes were wrong in this labyrinth. I repeated the exercise in the opposite direction, already with a resigned foreboding of failure. The geometry of the steel did not change: crossbars, beams, clamps, heavy joists . . . Halfway along I was struck by an appalling certainty: I was simply moving from one cage into another . . .

In fact, the grandstand's skeleton was nothing but a sequence of cages!

I nevertheless continued right to the end of this tough obstacle course, twisting this way and that, bending double, jumping, crawling flat on my face . . . At the other end of the grandstand—the same structure, the same trap, with spaces too narrow . . .

My panic caused the energy of a cornered wild beast to explode within me. I swung around, launched myself into a chaotic charge from one cage to the next, no longer noticing collisions with the flanges of beams, no longer headed in any particular direction . . . My forehead struck violently against the edge of a platform, my vision became blurred, I stopped and the pain brought me a wild calm, the gloomy acceptance of defeat.

Sunk in the torpor of a condemned man, I saw I was in a vast spider-web, spun from iron. This three-dimensional trellis was everywhere. The sky, the frozen earth, the shadow of the trees and the sun, everything was seen through a grid of solid bars, indifferent to my fevered presence.

My terror was so profound that, within this prison-like captivity, I must have glimpsed a more immense reality concerning the country I lived in, whose political character I was just beginning to grasp, thanks to snatches of conversation intercepted here and there . . . Much later the memory of this metallic straitjacket would make me think of my compatriots' despair in the face of ubiquitous censorship and police control and, above all, the impossibility of leaving the country, breaking through the armature of the Iron Curtain. All across that vast territory the same grandstands, the same slogans from loudspeakers, the same leaders' portraits. And beneath all the terraces, identical steel traps with no way out. I was not yet familiar with the concept of a "totalitarian regime." But the intimate sensation of what could be experienced in one took hold of me at that moment, in the chill bowels of that symbolic structure . . .

I resumed my journey with the numb movements of a sleepwalker, guided by the vague hope of slipping out beneath the lowest tier of the terraces, at the front of the grandstand. Now with each step I took I had to crouch a little lower. As I progressed toward this improbable way out, the cages became smaller. My calculation was not incorrect, the first tier, some fifteen inches from the ground, could have allowed me to slip through to the outside. But that took no account of the thickness of the ice, a black layer of which held the base of the skeleton in its grip. I lay full length upon the frozen surface, attempted to thrust my head under the bottom tier, which caused my shapka to fall off, with my cheek against the snow . . .

No, to escape, I would have had to grind away at that grainy crust or else cause it to melt. The idea of the thaw crossed my mind, but only to confirm the folly of such a notion: yes, remaining there until the fine weather in April . . .

I shook my head to rid myself of this vision and at that moment I saw a little spot of red encrusted in the ice. I touched it and recognized the remnant of a child's balloon, one of those that brought color to the grandstands during the two parades. The notables' children sometimes let them go, and, as we trod the asphalt in our enthusiastic ranks, we would watch these brightly colored bubbles vanishing into the depths of the sky . . . At that moment I was stretched out beneath the enclosure where they generally corralled such children and their mothers. The red balloon must have burst, fallen under the terraces, got caught on a beam . . .

I felt the gulf that separated me from the child who had lost it. I pictured a boy of my own age, living in a family, watching the parade, not in the middle of a crowd of strangers but on the grandstand, with his parents. I did not think, "a rich kid," it was more that I sensed the texture of a life so different from my own, a maternal presence at his side, the solidity of a mode of existence this boy would share with some other children in the enclosure. The impossibility of imagining his way of life coincided in my mind with my inability to escape from these steel cages.

Less surprised than before, I noticed the remnants of another balloon above me, blue, this one, dangling, caught between two bars. I reached up with my hand and . . .

It was like a shaft of light in the darkness: just where the collapsed balloon had been caught, the grandstand's metal supports formed crisscross patterns that, as the tiers rose higher, appeared to lead out into space!

It was a harsh challenge but hope gave me the strength of a daredevil. I had to lie flat on my stomach across the intersection of the bars, catch hold of the next crossover, haul myself up to its level, like a garment thrown over a fence, catch my breath, and, already feeling the pain of its sharp edges pressing into my diaphragm, resume this upward scramble.

Heave, balance a moment on a plank, wriggle like a lizard, grip again, thrust again . . .

The final lunge was performed with almost excessive vigor, with contempt for the vanquished monster. I gripped the highest bar, pivoted, grasped the topmost platform, straddled it, sat down upon the snow-covered timber.

I was free.

And blinded by light, my vision made iridescent by the effort. Deaf too, hearing only the drumming of the blood in my temples. After such a long incarceration everything seemed new to me, especially seen from this height. Tranquil sunlight, the whiteness of broad glades, the majestic calm of tall fir trees laden with snow.

On the pathway parallel to the river I was stunned to observe a little troop of children walking slowly away, all carrying shovels on their shoulders. I could see they were my comrades, including the girl we used to call "Red Riding Hood," on account of her hat, a pupil always in revolt against discipline, who was now moving along, apart from the others, and looked as if she were dancing as she went . . . So my absence had not been noticed and my interminable captivity in those steel cages had, in fact, lasted only a few minutes!

I began to make my way down the terraces, confused by these two strands of time, which made me doubt my own reality. And, as if to confirm the novelty of such a state of affairs, suddenly there was this young woman.

She had walked over to the grandstand, doubtless following our footprints in the drifts, had cleared snow from the end of one of the terraces, and was now sitting there, with closed eyelids, bathed in sunlight. On her knees she held an open book.

I halted in my descent, froze, aware that this occurrence did not belong to the world I lived in.

It was the first time an awareness of femininity had struck me so openly. Before that, women used to have the physique of the workers we came across in factories and on construction sites, strong women, often marked by physical labor and alcohol, whom life had molded to be able to hold their own against men. At the orphanage femininity was even less in evidence, we all of us, boys and girls, had a neutralized identity: our heads cropped once a month, clothes of the same thick flannel, a way of talking whose male roughness passed unnoticed. Of course there were those women assembled in the family enclosures on the grandstand, the wives of notables and apparatchiks, but they were as unreal as the symbolic figures on propaganda posters.

So, for me, the young woman I now saw became the first real woman. The slightly arched posture of her body was feminine. As was the knee, clad in the fine wool of a black stocking, left uncovered, with innocent and alarming naturalness, by the hem of her overcoat. And this face, her eyes shut, as if offered for a caress.

Thanks to her, I suddenly knew what it was to be in love: to forget your past life and exist only to sense the breathing of the one you love, the quiver of her eyelashes, the softness of her neck beneath a gray scarf. But, above all, to experience how blissfully impossible it was to reduce this woman simply to herself. For she was also the abundance of snow surrounding us and the glittering haze floating among the trees, and this whole moment in which there was already a foretaste of the hesitant breath of spring. She was all of this and each detail of her figure's mere outline echoed this far-reaching radiance.

The snow crunched under my foot, the woman opened her eyes, and I saw tears glistening upon her lashes. But her expression remained serene, almost glowing.

I climbed down, with sheepish caution, embarrassed to have disturbed her solitude. She lowered her head toward the book, an envelope had been slipped into it as a bookmark. In a hasty movement she closed the volume, as if I could have stolen the secret of her letter. At once she must have realized that a child, as taken aback by this unexpected encounter as herself, presented no threat. She looked at me for a long time, with a slight smile now. As I reached the lowest tier, I saw such a violently grief-stricken shadow pass across her gaze that I turned away and fled behind the grandstand.

There the mystery of the trap was resolved: one of the steel bars, simply held in place by a bolt, could be moved aside, and so gave access to the maze . . .

At the park's exit I passed two elderly women, members of the gardening staff, who were scraping halfheartedly at the frozen earth around some great stone basins. One of them inclined her head in the direction of the grandstand and gave a sigh: "Well, what can you say? . . . He was a submariner, her man. And if they're lost at sea they don't get a grave, or a cross . . ."

The other one stopped scraping, leaned on the handle of her shovel, and sighed as well: "Well, as for a cross, you know . . . Maybe it's better there's no grave. She'll get over it quicker . . ."

Catching these words in passing, I ran to rejoin my comrades. Unconsciously I was hoping to get back into our games, to forget the beauty and grief I had just experienced.

This forgetfulness never came. The young woman sitting on the snow-covered grandstand became much more than a memory. A way of seeing, of understanding, a tonality without which my life would not have been what it was to become. After my fleeting encounter with her I had a quite different perception of the weighty symbols celebrating my country's messianic project. All those parades, ceremonies, congresses, monuments . . . Curiously enough, I now had less desire to make fun of them, to criticize the hypocrisy of the dignitaries up there on the grandstand, to denounce them as profiteers for whom the dream of a new society was nothing more than a convenient old lie.

I sensed that the truth was to be found neither among them nor in the opposing camp, with the dissidents. I perceived it as simple and luminous, like that February day beneath the trees burdened with snow. The humble beauty of the woman's face with lowered eyelids showed up those platforms and their occupants and the pretentiousness of men prophesying in History's name as ridiculous. What spoke the truth was this woman's silence, her solitude, her love, so all-embracing that even this child, a stranger, scrambling down from tier to tier, remained forever dazzled by it.

This led me to the notion that this loving woman lived in a time that had no connection with the routine of our lives, so regularly punctuated by imposing mass spectacles. Or else, perhaps, that she lived in a world as it might have been without the overbearing aggressiveness of men, without grandstands, without the spiderwebs of their steel bars.

This hope revived in me my dream of the white city, of the men with new consciences, who, according to our teacher, would inhabit the future society. Yes, those fine, serene beings, who would not hoard and would work passionately for "the edification of the future" . . .

Then I became bewildered to realize that one thing was missing from this sublime enterprise.

"Love . . . ," an incredulous voice murmured within me. Everything was provided for in the ideal society: enthusiastic work by the masses, incredible advances in science and technology, the conquest of space, taking man into unknown galaxies, material abundance and rational consumption, linked to radical changes of attitude. Everything, absolutely everything! Except . . .

I did not think "love" again, I simply had a renewed vision of that young woman amid the great tranquillity of the snows bathed in sunlight. A woman with closed eyes and her face reaching out toward the one she loved.

Forty years later, when military secrets were made public, I learned the name of the submarine that had foundered at sea, carrying with it the man whose beloved ghost I had glimpsed on the face of the young woman seated on the parade grandstand. The events tallied: our encounter in the park had taken place just over a year after that disaster . . .

Now the story seemed clear, from start to finish. The only mystery that remained was this echo of both grief and serenity reflected in the young woman's expression. A superstitious fear held me back from putting words to this contradiction, I was afraid lest too much quibbling might destroy the frail beauty of the moment I had experienced as a child on top of the grandstand. With time this puzzlement came to form one of those nebulous memories we avoid clarifying, knowing it is the very haziness of our recollection that makes them dear to us. All I had to do to recall it was to pronounce these words, like a magic spell from my childhood: "She was the very first woman I fell in love with."

I would have been left with no more than this gentle echo from the past, had I not many years later encountered the same expression of a love, both radiant and tormented, in the eyes of another woman.

A town in the Var in southern France. I am passing through, between two trains, strolling rather at random. A winter's day, blinding with sunlight and the mistral, it feels as if the force of the blast is going to blow everything away in its shining fury. And everything takes off, the paper tablecloths and napkins on the café terraces, an old gentleman's hat, which he manages to pin to the ground with the help of his walking stick, plastic bags that become caught on the bare branches of plane trees, shutters that bang, the skirts of passing women's overcoats, which they thrust down against their buffeted bodies with the gestures of bullfighters . . . The wind's eddies of powdered emery hone the sun's rays, sharpen sounds. Car horns pierce the eardrums, snatches of words slice through the air in little fragments. The town is an old-fashioned photographer's magnesium flash.

My eyes dazzled, blinking with dust, I take refuge behind a wall and walk, almost groping my way, until I come upon gravestones and crosses. A cemetery, as white as the facades, but behind a row of cypress trees, sheltered from the wind, one can recover one's wits, breathe, turn one's back on the sun's relentless pounding, slow down again . . .

I am preparing to continue on my way, plunging back into the full force of wind and fire, when suddenly I see a dark smudge, motionless beside a gravestone. The smudge trembles, becomes the figure of a woman, turns, walks along beside the cypress hedge. A young face, eyes iridescent with tears . . . Drawing level with me, the woman gives me a faint smile and moves away toward the exit. When she is out of sight I go up to the grave she has just left, read the name, do a rapid calculation, alive for eighteen years before the year 2000, plus ten years after it. Twenty-eight. A husband? A fiancé? A brother? Dead the previous year . . .

In the street the sunlight's dazzling whiteness reminds me of a brilliant late winter's day in my native land. An unknown woman seated on that grandstand, profoundly calm, drowsing amid the snows. I have just rediscovered her face in the features of the young woman I passed in the cemetery. Her look of grief and serenity.

I realize this was a very fleeting moment, and yet a vital one in the life of a tortured being. All the pain is still there but love is already breaking free from it and is alive, briefly, in its absolute truth: the world, with its absurdities, its lies, and all its ugliness, no longer comes between the woman and the one she loves.

The world . . . I remember those steel cages where I flailed about as a child beneath the parade grandstand. And those drab hierarchs saluting the crowd. And the wars and revolutions, and the promises of global freedom and happiness that were proclaimed from the eastern frontier to the western. The thought plunges me into boundless amazement: nothing is left of it all!

At the end of the street I can still make out the young woman in black who has just walked away. An intense feeling of communion. Then her silhouette fades into the impetuous mistral's blue and gold.

THREE

⫿⫿⫿ ⫿⫿⫿ ⫿⫿⫿

The Woman Who Had Seen Lenin

First they introduced this man to us. He was in his fifties and very officially exploiting the fact of being one of History's elect. On Lenin's birthday, April 22, he was invited into the city's schools to talk to the pupils about his brief encounter with the Guide, the leader of the proletarian revolution. One morning, as part of his doubtless crowded touring schedule, he visited our orphanage.

Anticipating his coming was a source of great excitement for us. Without exaggeration, it was perhaps comparable to the sensation that might have been caused by the appearance in a late nineteenth-century French primary school of a veteran from Napoleon's Old Guard, whose fierce mustache had once brushed the emperor's chubby hand.

The man came in, smiled, spoke with amazing fluency, and indeed verve. He left pauses for us to give gasps of "Oh!" At suspense-filled moments in the narrative he spoke in a whisper. He was a professional. From the very start of his performance we were assailed by doubt.

In the first place he struck us as far too young. We had pictured a hoary, battle-scarred, bent old man. For, since he came from what, for us, was the dawn of time, the period of the 1917 revolution, he must necessarily have fought in the civil war and also the one against Hitler. Yes, we should have preferred a mustached grenadier, or at least the Russian version of this. But he had a smooth, pink baby's face and looked like the official image of a good little Komsomol apparatchik.

Our history teacher, a very pretty woman in her thirties, was herself taken aback by the visitor's youthful appearance.

"You don't look your age at all!" she exclaimed, her cheeks flushing slightly.

The man threw her a frankly saucy wink and murmured, "Ah, that's what comes of meeting so many beautiful teachers . . ."

Our doubts were only strengthened.

Could he have been a fraud? This possibility must be ruled out. Ideological education was a highly serious affair and the control exercised by the Party over public lectures of this type was too vigilant. Short of undergoing a lie detector test, the speaker would certainly have been the subject of detailed checks, biographical inquiries, personality tests. For the image of the founder of the State was no laughing matter. Every day in Lenin's life had been accounted for by an army of historiographers and so there would be no question of allowing an impostor to worm his way into it.

No, the man was not lying; he must truly have met the theorist of communism.

His rather youthful appearance was surprising, but, after all, if he was in his late fifties, purely as regards chronology, he could have been alive for a relatively brief period at the same time as Lenin. We were at the end of the sixties, so the man would have been born around 1910 to 1913. Lenin was able to get about without too much difficulty until 1922, before his illness immobilized him completely. The lecturer was nine years old, he told us, at the time of their historic encounter. So it was believable.

"The meeting was brief," he explained. "Vladimir Ilyich had come to our village to observe the implementation of the Party's policy of introducing machinery into rural life. The members of the local soviet were most eager to show him a new tractor. And it was during this demonstration that an appalling catastrophe loomed. It looked inevitable . . ."

The man's voice became muted, menacing. He frowned and his
nostrils flared, as if he had detected a criminal lurking among us. We
listened to him with bated breath, wondering what horrible mishap was
about to befall Lenin. We already knew the Guide had suffered an as-
sassination attempt and that in the old days the peasantry, the most
ignorant and backward of the working masses, refused to accept the benefits of collectivization. In conspiratorial tones the lecturer whispered,
"Although perfectly new, the tractor, the one the soviet was due to demonstrate to Lenin, broke down!"

A chill silence froze the class. At the age of twelve or thirteen we
were old enough to be aware of what happened to engineers incapable of
putting the Party's policies into practice. Under Stalin these "saboteurs"
were quickly sent to the camps. The pause, held by the lecturer for some
time, was intended to bring home to us the possibility of such an outcome. If at this stage in his narrative, he had proclaimed, "So Lenin gave
orders for them all to be shot!" I believe we would not have been enor-
mously surprised. We might even have applauded such an action, harsh
but contributing to the achievement of collectivization . . . Today such
a reaction in the children we were then would seem unbelievably cruel.
But in those days we lived in a world in which there were enemies everywhere to be unmasked. The indoctrination we underwent, often without
our being aware of it, was based upon the hatred of a broad category of
human beings hostile to the welfare of our country. Depending on the
historical context, the Party decided which of our fellow men fell into
this category. More realistically, after all, the consequences of the Nazi
invasion were still present in everyone's memories, and in the bodies of
many war wounded . . .

The storyteller's voice, somber until then, suddenly became animated and emotional: "So, by way of encouragement, Lenin asked the
mechanic to explain what was not working. Moved to tears by Vladimir
Ilyich's friendly tones, he started to answer his questions. And that's how,
guided by the great Lenin's constantly judicious probing, he identified
the cause of the problem. Within fifteen minutes the engine was running.

The plow, drawn by the tractor, was digging its first furrow. The first furrow of the new life!"

The man clapped his hands together to trigger our dutiful applause. His story was faultlessly constructed. The best juggler in a circus is not the one who immediately demonstrates perfection, but that rare ace who, as he sets ten objects dancing in the air, allows one or two of them to fall so that the public can sense how difficult a feat it is. To whet their curiosity and increase the tension. And at length, when the spectators are beginning to doubt his skill, hey presto! all his playthings pirouette rhythmically in the air together, without a hitch. Our lecturer had used the same device: a tractor goes on strike, all hope seems to be lost, and suddenly the Guide steps in and a miracle occurs. At least that is how we perceived it, because for our generation Lenin remained a cross between a mythical hero and a wonder worker. A benevolent spirit, a just and indulgent grandfather, very different from the ferocious Stalin, whose infamous crimes had recently been acknowledged by the Party and who, as the lecturer hinted, would doubtless have thrown the mechanic into prison.

We applauded, but our hearts were not in it. His performance had been "over the top," as we would say nowadays. For this "man who had seen Lenin" was a fairground barker, a ham actor, a spin doctor for official History . . . He sailed out of the classroom with the lithe aplomb of a pop singer, a winning smile on his lips, and another wink at our beautiful history teacher.

We were a long way from that austere veteran of Napoleon's Old Guard, tanned by the smoke of battle.

Disillusionment caused a group of pupils, of whom I was one, to linger in the classroom. We surrounded the teacher, upset, puzzled.

"He was a bit too . . . too neat and tidy," one of my comrades ventured.

This description, at first sight out of place (in fact, somewhat untidily used), nevertheless expressed the truth: yes, a man too meticulous, too smooth, lacking the bitter stench of History.

Our teacher decoded the thought behind it and quickly came to the rescue lest we lose our faith.

"Listen," she murmured, as if sharing a confidence. "There's something you have to understand. When he met Lenin he was a child, so, naturally, when he recalls this today it rejuvenates him . . . But look, I know, well, not exactly personally, an elderly lady . . . who was very close to Lenin and used to see him when he lived in Switzerland and France . . . She lives in a village about twenty miles from the city. I'll try to do some research and discover her precise address . . ."

The old lady's home was not easy to locate. It was not until halfway through June that our teacher gave us the name of the village, Perevoz, which could be reached by taking a little train that served a string of sub-urbs, hamlets, and simple stops giving access to forestry sites. She even showed us a black-and-white photograph in a big book, where we saw a woman of mature years with powerfully molded features and great, dark eyes. Her posture, both imposing and voluptuous, was evocative of the physical suppleness of Oriental women. Many years later I would realize that she resembled the famous portrait of the aging George Sand . . .

Since the lecturer's visit most of the pupils had had time to forget about such ghosts from the revolutionary era, and on the day of the expedition there were only six of us to go. To cap it all, as no other boy wanted to come, I found myself in the company of five girls.

For them this outing represented a significant social event, we had never before set out to visit someone who did not belong to the closed world of the orphanage. I noticed they had got hold of some lipstick and had blackened their lashes and eyelids. It is well known that girls of their age mature quickly. I felt like a page boy at a wedding with five brides to escort. On the outward journey, fortunately, the train was almost empty.

More knowing than I, they must have sensed that there was something intriguing about this sudden appearance of a woman at Lenin's side. The Guide, that completely asexual being, was all at once acquiring disturbing psychological depths that brought him mysteriously to life, much more substantially than the mummy on display in his mausoleum in Red Square, although that was real. It was like picturing a statue of Lenin starting to stir, making eyes, ready to reveal his intimate secrets to us.

At the address we were given in the village of Perevoz, we found a long single-story building lined with flower beds where mainly weeds were growing. The walls were painted a very pale blue, the shade of corn-flowers on the brink of fading, losing their color.

There was clearly some mistake, it was impossible for "the woman who had known Lenin" to be living in such a dump. We rang the bell and, after a wait, pricking up our ears at the slightest rustle, pushed open the door . . .

The interior presented an even more wretched appearance: a long, dark corridor with little windows along one side, doors on the other, it looked like a barracks or a home for single women. Even our orphan-age seemed to us more welcoming than this impersonal lodging. The shadowy depths were lit by a feeble bare bulb and a voice both weary and aggressive shouted out: "She's not here. Gone to the city. Don't know when she'll be back . . ."

A housekeeper or caretaker appeared. We repeated the name of the lady we were looking for, certain we would now be given the correct address.

"Yes, that's her," the caretaker replied, "room nine. But she's not here, I tell you. She's at her son's, in Moscow. Come back in a month . . ."

She stepped forward, ushering us gently toward the exit.

Disconcerted, we made a tour of the building, which might have seemed uninhabited had we not noticed ancient, wrinkled faces at two or three windows, peering out at us between a couple of pots of geraniums. It was a painful discovery: "the woman who had seen Lenin" was ending her days among these faded ghosts! It was rather like a den of witches . . .

Not really downhearted, the girls decided to look on the bright side: "Well, at least we can have a smoke here, without the supervisors getting on our backs."

They lit up their cigarettes and strutted along the village street like film stars who had just arrived in the back of beyond. A single street, wooden houses with collapsed roofs, a feeling of great neglect, of life on the verge of extinction. It was a gray day; occasionally a gust of wind ran through the dense foliage with a hasty, plaintive whisper . . .

Only one inhabitant deigned to view the five young beauties: a man, obviously drunk, sitting in the open window of his izba. He wore a faded undershirt over a body all blue with tattoos. As the divas walked past, his unevenly bearded cheeks creased into a somewhat unnerving grin. And all at once, in an astonishingly fine voice, he recited:

> On a marble island lapped by an azure sea
> A sorceress waits, in her castle's gilded glow,
> At ease each night beneath a spreading tree,
> She weeps and calls me . . .

"Well, she can go fuck herself beneath her tree!" he concluded abruptly, giving my brides a sneering look.

All at once he disappeared, as if he had fallen backward onto the floor, the way figures somersault out of sight in a puppet show.

Hurriedly the girls retreated toward me, their only defender.

"The train's at four twenty. We're going back," they said, reconciled to the failure of their fashion parade. "We'll wait in the station café. It'll be more fun there than in this hole. There's no point in hanging around here. That friend of Lenin's won't come now, that's for sure."

"I'm going to stay. I know she'll come."

"Well, watch out. The four twenty's the last train. Don't miss it or those old witches'll bite off your . . . ears, ha, ha, ha!"

They set off toward the station; the street became empty, a cigarette stub lay smoking in the dust. I hesitated, then walked back to the blue building. This time no faces appeared at the row of windows half covered by weeds. The inmates had probably just gathered in the dining room. Or did each one eat lunch in her own room?

Hesitating over what tactics to employ, I pushed open the front door and found myself face-to-face with the caretaker at a table. She had opened her little lodge and was having a meal there. I particularly noticed a bottle of wine placed on the floor, behind one of the table legs, which would make it possible to conceal this solitary libation in the case of an unexpected visit from a superior. I knew the label on the bottle: a poor-quality wine, a rotgut people referred to as "ink" because it was so dark, the color of walnut stain.

The caretaker recognized me easily (a boy among five girls!), and instead of the rebuff I was expecting, her greeting was almost affectionate: "No, she's still not come back, our poor lady . . . Oh yes, that's the truth: she's a poor lady . . ." Her gaze clouded over with a veil of melancholy. I believe she had just reached the stage of intoxication that, for a while, makes us soft, forgiving, understanding.

"Come on then, have a bite to eat!" she invited me, noticing how hungrily I was swallowing my saliva. She offered me bread; cut me a slice of sausage. Then, with a hefty movement of her foot, pushed a little stool toward me and watched me eating with a sympathetic air.

"Oh yes, she's poor, all right!" she exclaimed after a moment, as if I had expressed reservations about the truth of her remarks. "Not because she's been dumped here in this shack. When you're old you don't need a palace. No, it's that . . . she's got nobody who loves her . . ."

The caretaker sniffed, wiped her eyes on the sleeve of her blouse, spoke in a broken voice: "Oh, she did have a husband . . . But he ratted on her, the bastard. It was after the war. Before you were born. She was arrested and her husband disowned her to save his own skin. He even denounced her. Said she was an enemy of the people and a . . . What do they call it? . . . A cosmo . . . a conso . . . Anyway he said she wasn't patriotic, you know. And he divorced her. They had a daughter and a son. When Stalin died they let her out, but no one in the family wanted to have anything to do with her anymore. Her husband had married another woman long ago. And her children were in good jobs in Moscow. They were ashamed of their mother, her being fresh out of prison. And what's more, she hadn't a penny and nowhere to live . . . Look what she gave me as a present . . ."

The caretaker thrust her hand into a drawer, took out a pretty round comb, and slipped it into her hair with a young girl's coquetry. Then, catching a look of amazement in my gaze, she quickly removed the comb and gabbled on in haste, to conclude her story: "She gets a pauper's pension but she's ready to part with her last kopeck. Even to Sashka, who's our singer here and tattooed worse than a savage . . . Right, that's it. On your way now! That's enough talk. I've told you already, she's not here and I don't know when she'll be back. In any case, she never talks about Lenin. Go on. Away with you!"

Suddenly in a bad temper, she stood up, giving me little thumps on my back to direct me toward the door. I guessed she needed another draft of alcohol to restore her to the level of intoxication that fills our hearts with floods of benevolence.

I left both better informed and less certain of what I knew. "The woman who had seen Lenin" thrown into prison! Forgotten by her nearest and dearest. Sharing her meager funds with a tattooed drunkard . . . All this was a long way from our history textbooks and the yarn that fresh-faced mountebank of a lecturer had spun us.

Disconcerted, I loitered for a moment in the village's empty street, walked past the drunkard Sashka's house, went as far as the edge of a wood that extended down into a broad valley covered in meadowland that had not been threatened with scything for a long time. A combine harvester, brown with rust, all its tires flat, lay idle there, surrounded by a profusion of grasses and flowers. There was a silence now, as if settled by the imminence of rain. Even the birds had stopped singing. My own presence was painful to me; I felt I had strayed into a time well before my own life. I decided to go back to the station, rejoin my five brides.

As I walked past the blue building I had an idea that whetted my curiosity. "The woman who had seen Lenin" lived in room nine. Room

one was located just next door to the caretaker's lodge. And, as there
was only one window per room, it would be easy to locate room nine.
Proud of my deduction, I slipped along beside the wall like a thief,
crouching low and glancing rapidly into each room: numbers one, two,
three, four . . .

I was certain that in room nine, the very last in the row, I should see
a portrait of Lenin, possibly even photographs of him in the company of
the lady we were looking for.

Slowly, with a pounding heart, I peered in at the window opening.
First I saw a narrow worktable, or rather a desk, on which a few books, a
pen, and a stack of paper were arranged in perfect order. One of the vol-
umes lay open, pencil marks on the page showed signs of an interrupted
reading . . . then there was a bed, a blanket drawn tight, military fashion . . . A very simple lamp of an antiquated type. And finally a portrait.
It was not Lenin. A young man, dressed in the uniform of a cavalryman
in the Red Army, a long cape and this cap, with its design based on a
medieval helmet, the famous *budyonovka* . . .

The woman was not there, the caretaker had not lied. No longer
hiding, I became glued to the window, feeling as if I were looking into
a display cabinet in a museum showing the reconstruction of a way of
life in a remote past. All the little space was filled with books and the
remainder of the walls covered in photographs. Views of places where
the architecture was very unlike that of our Russian towns. Group
portraits, a color verging on ocher, static poses that gave away just how
old the snapshots were . . .

And then this photograph: a young woman with long, dark hair,
a mother holding a child in her arms whose gaze was curiously directed
to one side.

"Does that interest you?"

I gave a start, backing away abruptly from the window and colliding with the person who had just called out to me. I turned around,
openmouthed, trying to find excuses, explanations. An adolescent girl,
scarcely older than myself, was staring at me fearlessly, but also without

hostility, which gave me courage and left me time to study her: a mass of raven hair tied back with a scarlet ribbon, big, dark eyes, and a rather grown-up air that, mysteriously, seemed familiar to me . . . I hastened to give high-sounding reasons for my espionage. "It's for our history lessons. I'd like to meet the woman who'd seen Lenin . . ."

"So would I," the girl cut in. "And it's not the first time I've come here. But she's never at home . . . My name's Maya."

I introduced myself, a little awkwardly, sensing that she belonged to a world where dealings between men and women, children and adults, were more relaxed thanks to codes of politeness my comrades either knew nothing of or regarded as signs of weakness.

We moved away from the blue building, walking slowly, following the village's only street. I felt quite ill at ease, nervous lest I let slip one of those coarse expressions that made up our daily language at the orphanage, grasping, too, that an invisible bond had just been created between this girl and me and that I must be worthy of such a gift from fate. This Maya had a radiant beauty that, from minute to minute, became more magical, almost heartbreakingly so, still hinting at a hidden resemblance to a face I could not identify in my memory. On top of all this the time for the train was close and I was already picturing myself appearing with this new companion in front of my five brides. Their mockery, the teasing glances the passengers would give me in the midst of my harem . . .

Maya's voice gradually calmed my fears. Hers was a more serious voice than the tones one might expect from a girl of thirteen or fourteen. More melancholy, too.

"This woman who'd seen Lenin is called Alexandra Guerdt. Her brother was killed in the First World War. After that she had only one dream: to rid the earth of rulers who send young men to their deaths, starve their peoples, and rob the weak. It was a dream of worldwide brotherhood, shared happiness. During the tsarist era she remained abroad, in Europe. That was where she met Lenin. He admired her greatly. He even entrusted her with a number of secret missions. They wrote special letters to one another, with an ordinary text, but, between the lines, words written in milk. Yes, milk! You had to hold the paper over a flame and then the words appeared . . . After the revolution she worked on his staff. She lived with a man who'd been a major in the Red Army cavalry. At the end of the thirties he was accused of treason and shot. As they weren't married she only spent two years in prison. She was released because the war against Hitler had just started. She spoke several languages, German in particular. Stalin decided she could be useful . . . But then, after the war, she got another sentence, at the time of the struggle against cosmopolitanism . . ."

"Eh? Com-so-politism? What's that? Political Komsomols?"

"No, it's . . . well, there were people who were suspected of not loving their country enough. And that was when her husband (she'd met him during the war) disowned her. And worst of all, he brought up his children to despise their mother. She was too shaken by her life in the camps to put up a fight. She lived alone now. Many years later her innocence was recognized. They even returned her Party card and historians wrote about her. Then her family wanted to get back in touch. But she always refused . . ."

We reached the spot where the old combine lay dormant. The sky on that June day had become even more gray, and the wind was sweeping through the trees with a sad, autumnal sound. It was time to go back to the station. Maya was silent, her gaze lost in the distant mist over the fields, and from time to time she shook her head gently, as if expressing some refusal in a reverie where I no longer had any place. Yet I so much wanted to exist for her! I must attempt a subterfuge, which is why, in genial and flattering tones, and with a click of my tongue, I exclaimed, "Hey! You're a real ace at history. I bet you've read a lot of books . . ."

She roused herself, gave me a vague smile, and murmured, "Not all that many. And in the books, you know, the woman who'd seen Lenin is given the name she assumed as a young revolutionary. The name I told you, her real name, Alexandra Guerdt . . . not many people know that."

She fell silent again and I sensed a cord within her stretched to breaking point. Her voice resonated with a musical quality, close to tears:

"I know the name, you see, because Alexandra Guerdt, she's . . . my grandmother."

She did not burst out sobbing but her breath came in gasps as she tried to speak: "I've got cousins who live in your city. But my family lives in Moscow. I lied to my parents. I told them I wanted to spend a week with my uncle and aunt. This was all so as to be able to come here, to Perevoz. Today's my last day. Tomorrow I go back to Moscow. I've never been able to meet my grandmother. My father says she's an old madwoman. And this village, you've seen it. What a wilderness! I've asked the caretaker a hundred times. She sent me packing. And she's lying, in any case. I don't know where my grandmother could be. She's too old for long journeys and besides . . . She's really very poor."

We were walking back up the street toward the station. The drunkard's window was wide open. I quickened the pace to protect Maya from defilement by oaths or smutty rhymes. But it was from behind a row of raspberry canes that Sashka called out to us, and this time his powerful voice was tinged with a strange lassitude.

"Get along home now. You'll never see her, our good Alexandra. She's not for the likes of two-faced bastards like you. As soon as any meddlers poke their noses in, she locks the door and goes off quick down the valley. She knows the timetables. They come on the midday train, all the stupid pricks who want to see her, and go back on the four twenty. I know the timetables, too. That's all I do know. So piss off now and leave us in peace."

He disappeared as abruptly as the first time.

Dumbfounded, we stood there face-to-face for a moment, then, with unspoken accord, we started to run toward the valley.

Just beyond the wreck of the combine harvester the meadow sloped more steeply. From above, beyond the thickets, the banks of a stream could be seen and, amid the willows, a footpath swamped with wild plants. A dark figure, still very far away, was walking slowly along the bank, coming toward the village. Despite the distance I could make out the ample chignon of white hair, an imposing, upright stature. In a fraction of a second the whole tale I had just heard, this tragic life story that had spanned the century, was condensed into a human presence.

"Go down, Maya! You must go down to her. Don't wait for her here. Run!"

My whisper was on fire with emotion.

"No, I'm scared," she muttered. "I can't. She'll never want to see me. She'll drive me away. I can't!"

I saw tears welling in her eyes.

"Yes, you can. You've got to. But you must go down to her. Go on!"

I grasped her by the arm to pull her along. She resisted.

"All right. Please yourself. You're chicken! A little Moscow bitch! Well, I've got my train to catch. I'm not going to waste my time on a dope like you."

Turning my back on her, I ran flat out toward the village.

I turned around once, near the combine. Lower down in the valley I saw Maya embarked on a wild descent, her ribbon had vanished, her hair, untied, flailed about her shoulders. And farther on, at the heart of an endless green-and-silver plain, a very tall old lady was waiting there, where the path climbed the hill.

Then, with all my being, I felt I was wildly, desperately in love. Not only with Maya and her dark locks flying in the wind as she ran. But also with the plants that swayed as she passed, and with that gray, sad sky and the air that smelled of rain. I was even in love with that old piece of farm machinery with flat tires, sensing that it was quite essential to the harmony that had just been created before my eyes . . .

I arrived five minutes after the due time but the train was late. The crowd was waiting on the platform, tightly packed, ready to pile in, hoping to find seats. Near the station building, through the comings and goings of the passengers, I saw the drunkard Sashka, sitting on the ground. He was much older than I had thought. Gray locks clung to his brow. He was singing, his eyes almost closed. His tattoos could not be seen for he had put on a jacket with several medals from the last war pinned to its front . . .

When the train came in the people surged forward toward the track, Sashka was left alone, I threw him a farewell glance and suddenly saw that both his legs were amputated. A dusty cap was flung down in front of his stumps. A pair of crutches stood there, leaning against the station wall. As the crowd rushed into the carriages he recited the verses I had already heard:

> On a marble island lapped by an azure sea
> A sorceress waits, in her castle's gilded glow,
> At ease each night beneath a spreading tree,
> She weeps and calls me! I shall never go . . .

During the summer we worked far away from the city, as we used to every year, on construction sites and on kolkhozes in the fields. At the end of August, the day of our return to the orphanage, a supervisor handed me a letter that had been waiting for me since June. The only one I had ever received throughout my childhood. Mail personally addressed to a pupil constituted a notable event, exceptional even, and must have aroused some curiosity. The envelope had been opened and the contents doubtless read. But it contained nothing secret. Some news of the capital, the account of a film Maya had just seen with a girlfriend . . . She had signed it with a single *M* and, in essence, was simply writing to send me good wishes for the holidays.

I was boundlessly happy and, at the same time, terribly disappointed: words so precious and so dull! And also, this bizarre short sentence as a postscript, her advice to me to drink milk. Milk? Very well, I would be sure to drink some milk.

The next day, rereading her letter for the hundredth time, I saw the light: milk! Poor fool, how could I have failed to understand at once?

That evening I assembled all I needed: a stub of candle, some matches, a magnifying glass. I hid behind a shed in the orphanage yard and after checking that no troublesome person might interfere with my clandestine activities, I immersed myself in a labor of alchemy. The candle glowed, the flame heated the paper, which slowly began to reveal the hidden message. The faintly yellowed outlines of the words traced by a pen dipped in a drop of milk began to appear, barely visible but decipherable all the same.

Maya wrote: "Now I know why Alexandra Guerdt wouldn't talk about her past anymore. In the civil war she worked in Lenin's secretariat. One day she read a telegram he'd just dictated to be sent to a political commissar. A town was resisting the authority of the Soviets. Lenin said he should kill '100–1000' people, as an example. The number was indicated just like that, with a dash. Yes, Lenin was ordering the execution of between a hundred and a thousand men, by way of reprisal, just as the commissar thought fit . . . Alexandra was furious: a pencil stroke wiping out hundreds of living beings. They laughed in her face. She stormed out . . . Today she believes the fraternal world she dreamed of was also destroyed by that dash . . . I hope to see you again one day. On a marble island, perhaps! And don't forget, really, to drink some milk. Maya."

All through my life, in calling Alexandra Guerdt to mind, I have never been able to picture her unhappy. Quite the contrary, those summer days long ago were suffused with a profound joy, patient and calm, in a remote village where, for me, she still existed. So much so that the very concept of earthly happiness has come to find its incarnation in a muted June day, the pale expanse of an immense valley with tall plants and a very young girl's headlong descent toward an elderly woman breaking into a gentle smile.

FOUR

An Eternally Living Doctrine

The fatal mistake we make is looking for a paradise that endures. Seeking pleasures that do not grow stale, lasting attachments, embraces with the vigor of lianas: the tree dies but their enveloping tracery continues verdant. This obsession with what lasts causes us to overlook many a fleeting paradise, the only kind we can aspire to in the course of our lightning journey through this vale of tears. These often make their dazzling appearance in places so humble and ephemeral that we refuse to linger there. We prefer to fashion our dreams from the granite blocks of whole decades. We believe we are destined to live as long as statues.

The paradise that taught me not to take myself for a statue was located in a place difficult to define. An intermediate space between a vast industrial zone and a scrap of an old village that was dying before the onset of a titanic building development: vast concrete structures, steel cylinders thrusting toward the sky, a tangle of thick pipes, the circulatory system that fed the machinery and tanks whose hubbub and hissing could be heard behind the walls.

After lessons on those sunny days in March, I used to walk through a suburb surrounded by railroad lines, pass beneath a broad, dark viaduct, continue beside factory walls, and, following the rusty tracks that led to an old boat landing on the Volga, arrive at this spot it is hard to find a name for. Six or seven izbas, the remnants of orchards, an abandoned barn that spoke of agricultural activity long ago. Somewhat closer to the river a warehouse in ruins, the relic of a little fishing port.

I would head toward a house with two low windows facing the street that reflected the sparkle of the snow in the sunlight and addressed me with a look full of resigned wisdom. A girl, aged about fifteen, like me, was waiting for me at the door; visitors were rare in this remote corner, she could see me from a long way off. I sensed the snowy chill lingering over her body beneath her indoor dress. The distance that lay between us—those last few dozen yards—seemed to me to be at once infinite and nonexistent.

We greeted one another with a simple nod, a quick smile, without shaking hands, without kissing. And nothing happened during the two or three hours that we were together. None of what might have been expected by way of physical bonding, according to the notions of today's world.

We would talk about a novel in which a couple of young adventurers discovered the underwater entrance to Atlantis on one of the Cape Verde islands. We would laugh when a book on our study program struck us as too stupid (one somewhat visionary author declared that the completion of a five-year plan within four years would speed up time throughout the universe). We stayed silent a lot, especially me, without feeling the least bit embarrassed by it. Words were superfluous, for there was this slipping away of the light that would slowly transform the dazzling March afternoon, from the moment when I arrived, into a mauve dusk, signaling the time for me to leave. There was the tranquillity of this little house with two rooms, its extreme cleanliness, the sleep-inducing tick of an old clock. A calm, completely indifferent to the close proximity of the monstrous factory, to the road where batches of huge trucks hurtled along, to all the brutal, busy, thunderous life that threatened the little village in the depths of its snowy silence. There was the happiness of being together, certain that at every moment we were living through the very essence of what life could be here in this world.

Every time I came from the city I would see enormous red letters mounted on the factory roof, characters cast in concrete, each of them probably ten feet high, spelling out a sentence whose length indicates the dimensions of the building: "Long live Marxism-Leninism, an eternally living, creative, revolutionary doctrine!" The end of the sentence became lost in the smoke that hung over that industrial site, but the walls continued well beyond the slogan, right out as far as the misty stretch of wasteland and the forest's gray fringe . . .

I was enthralled by this doctrine, which they taught us at school. It put into words what I had previously only been able to picture in a reverie: a white city bathed in sunlight, fraternal men freed at last of all hatred, united by an awe-inspiring plan that carried them toward a radiant future. And also the vision, rashly sketched by our history teacher, of stores bursting with plenty, from which the citizens of the future would take only what was strictly necessary . . . These childish dreams were now illuminated by the brilliance of texts studied in the classroom, among them *The Communist Manifesto*, which gave us a glimpse of a world not yet realized, from which brutish rivalry between men, the violence of exploitation, the carnivorous greed of property owners, all these congenital malformations of the tribes of humanity, would be banished. Each day torrents of words in the newspapers or on the radio sought to convince us that this promised future lay at the end of a new five-year plan. Each day reality belied these promises. At length people no longer noticed the letters ten feet high on the factory roof.

And while I so longed to believe in this fraternal world, I knew that when you passed through our city's suburbs at night it was better to have a switchblade in your pocket.

Once I set foot on the street leading to the village I forgot about these contradictions. In the distance, on the doorstep of the house closest to the river, I could see my friend's pale dress and time took on an altered significance, becoming estranged from the life I had just left behind. The street lined with blue snowdrifts detached itself from reality, slipped by me in a silent progress like those in cities in our dreams, which we recollect with incredulous joy as we leave them on waking. From the river came the echoing rustle of ice floes beginning to melt. The chilly, intoxicating scent of the waters breaking free, still invisible beneath the snows, hung on the air. The sun dazzled me and at first I could not manage to bring into focus the well-loved face that was smiling at me. I blinked, unconsciously sensing that the problem was not just with the sun but with human eyesight's inability to see beyond the fine features to the elusive beauty being born and reborn at every instant . . .

We went in, my friend made some tea, words came or not, the silence of the house was enough for us. Sometimes we listened, but at an almost inaudible volume, to Tchaikovsky's *Seasons*. It was always the same section, "June," which my friend located with a conjurer's deftness on a large, tired long-playing record. We never turned up the sound, the music was intended only as a faint murmur, it seemed more secret like that, beyond the reach of the life that carried on in the distance, with its din, its pointless speed, its deafness.

The light painted the passing hours, changing from gold to amber, then turning pale.

We used to talk about our first meeting, a source of inexhaustible amusement. A month earlier, before we knew one another, we had taken part in paramilitary training where several schools in the city formed two opposing armies. Assaults on fortresses built from ice blocks, hurling practice grenades, field exercises in a park. The bellicose tension was more than playful: we fought ferociously, seeking, for the duration of a war game, to emulate the pantheon of patriotic heroes. The army our orphanage belonged to wore green armbands, our enemies yellow armbands . . . The light was beginning to fade when I gave chase to a patch of yellow running away into the undergrowth. To capture a prisoner alive was held to be a far more glorious exploit than riddling him with imaginary bullets and shouting, "Lie down, you're dead!" I caught up with the fugitive in a clearing, knocked him over by pushing him violently in the back, and thrust my plastic pistol against the nape of his neck. The enemy turned around. It was a girl. I hesitated, then helped her up. We paused for a moment, uncertain whether to resume our roles or instead . . .

The noise of the battle was now coming from a long way off, almost blotted out by the calm of the great trees asleep under the snow. The warlike passion that had animated us a moment earlier was dissipated in the fading air of a winter dusk, in the silence marked by the two of us panting breathlessly.

"They were supposed to come this way . . . ," the girl murmured, making it clear to me that the same notion had occurred to us both, the real possibility of calling a halt to this cruel and childish game, this training in brute force, and recognizing that quite a different mode of existence, quite a different world, lay close at hand . . .

My prisoner's face had a simple beauty, somewhat austere, or at least avoiding any facile charm, one of those whose fine features, when first seen, impose an attitude, a tone of voice, a respect for the sovereign mystery of that person.

"My name's Vika," she said, while I, for my part, made nervous by the direction our encounter was taking, introduced myself in a highly military manner, starting with surname, then my first name, as we did at roll call in the orphanage.

"Reporting for duty, sir!" she replied with a smile and we moved off, without hurrying, in the direction of the shouts of delight announcing the victory of one or other of the camps.

Knowing which side had won that evening became a matter of indifference to us . . . Mentally I was pronouncing that name, Vika, like the first word of an unknown language.

Nowadays people would refer, with a sly grin, to the understanding we had as a "platonic relationship." The description seems appropriate enough: no physical bonding arose between us during the very brief period of our friendship. Yet that term is also utterly misleading, since at no time during my presence in the little house near the old port did this "issue" concern us. For it was never an issue. We were far from being particularly prudish. At the orphanage, amid the crowding together of the two sexes and several age groups, there was not much I did not know about the joys and sorrows of the human body. My prisoner was probably as well acquainted with them as I was. Soviet society at that time, under cover of an official coyness, was relatively relaxed. But, without our imposing any kind of vow of chastity upon ourselves, we expressed our love in other ways.

For us the fact of being in love went without saying. But rather than provoking a state of feverish excitement, it made us almost impassive. We became slow, hypnotized by the novelty and power of what was happening to us. I could spend hours in perfect felicity, all it took was the occasional movement of the pale dress through the room bathed in the copper glow of the March sun. To see a lightly curled plait, every hair gleaming as a ray of light picked it out, was sufficient for me to feel happy. And when those eyes, tinged with green and blue, rested upon me, I felt I was starting to exist in an identity that was truly my own at last.

At that age, when our lives seem endless, I could easily have given away half of the span that was left for me to have the certainty, expressed in one sweet word, of being loved. Doubtless that word would have destroyed the very essence of the hypnotic bliss we were both immersed in. If our relationship had lasted longer, words would, in any case, have come . . . But in the absence of any such declaration I remained mutely adoring, noting the gestures traced by a hand in motion, the fluttering of eyelashes, the depth of an intake of breath, relishing the chill of the snows when, in the evening, my friend came out onto the house's little front steps to say good-bye to me and follow me with her eyes as far as the corner. These were silent signs, but when we gaze at the stars, do we not, like Rimbaud, hear their "soft rustling sound" quite clearly?

And then came a declaration much more unexpected than those words whose tenderness I at once hoped for and dreaded.

That day the mounting spiral of the petty cares of existence seemed to be doing all it could to give the lie to the slogan I used to read on the factory roof when I went to the village, with its "eternally living, creative, revolutionary doctrine." I had a swollen lip, the result of a quarrel, a brief and violent one, as our scuffles at the orphanage always were: an abrupt upsurge of hatred, fists raw from the exchange of blows, the conviction that one could kill . . . Then there was a bus, packed with bodies crushed against one another, people on the way home to their suburbs, exhausted workmen, aggressive, ready to exchange insults and tear one another to pieces at the slightest jolt of that scrap metal on wheels. "Fraternity . . . The radiant future . . . ," I said to myself bitterly. And just beside the stop where I got off four drunkards were fighting, trading soft, clumsy blows, trampling on the one who fell over, falling over beside him . . .

The sun threw glaring light on the factory roof with its monumental message of the "eternally living doctrine." A voice within me was yelling and weeping.

I turned the corner into the village street and from a long way off I could see the faint patch of a dress lit up by the blue luminescence of the snow. An invisible frontier, compounded of this brilliance and the icy scent of the river, separated me from the world of a moment ago. Only the taste of blood in my mouth reminded me of where I had come from.

We often used to go for a walk among the old izbas of the village, strolling down toward the boat landing, toward the shore. Sensing that an unaccustomed tension was mounting within the dreamy calm of our tête-à-tête, we did so that day . . .

The mild warmth of March had woven a filigree of melting sheets of ice, lacy rose windows. As I snatched them up they shattered in my hands, just as my friend was noticing their star-studded beauty. We walked down a slope of virgin snow, punctuated only with birds' footprints. Sinking up to our knees, we could feel the little lumps of ice working their way into our shoes.

Like an abandoned raft, the old jetty lay amid the pack ice. It was attached by rusty cables to the stumps of steel posts embedded in the bank. We climbed onto this wreck and with incredulous joy touched the surface of the planks: they were already dry and warm from having been exposed to the sun all day. Beneath a partially collapsed lean-to a bench stood waiting for the ghosts of former travelers. We sat down facing the white immensity of the still-sleeping river, our gaze lost in the distance, and gradually recovered the slow pulse of the happiness that always used to set the rhythm for our encounters.

That day such serenity no longer seemed enough for me. The bitterness I had been storing up since the morning gave me a longing for some vast, radical change, a revolution that would wipe away the hatred from the world's countenance and from all those grimacing faces I had come across on my way to the village: those of the men and women crammed together in the bus, and before that, at the orphanage, the boy who had punched me in the face, his gleeful guffaw at the sight of my blood. But also the somber mass of workers whom the factory swallowed up every morning and spat out in the evening, a lava of drained bodies and lackluster looks. The march of History toward the promised future, toward that ideal city where men would at last become worthy of the name, must be speeded up.

For the first time I spoke about this to my friend. I got up from the bench, gesticulating, my enthusiasm growing the more my talking about it made the dream seem close and achievable. Yes, a fraternal society, a way of life that would exclude aggression and greed, a plan that would bond together everyone's goodwill, at present fettered by the pettiness of individualism. I think I also talked about the disappearance of the State, for which there would be no need, since all men would form a single community, in which police, army, and prisons would be superfluous. I knew Lenin had promised this in his vision of the future . . . That was it, a community of men destined for happiness!

"But aren't you happy now?" Vika asked suddenly.

The question threw me.

"Er . . . Yes . . . But I'm not talking about myself. What I meant, you see, was that . . . in general, this new society will allow other people to lead lives of joy . . ."

"I don't understand. All these people you want to bring happiness to in the future. What's to stop them being happy now? Not hating other people, not being greedy, like you said. Not punching other people in the face, at any rate . . ."

"Well . . . you see . . . I don't think they know the true path yet. They need to be shown. They need to be given a plan, a theory . . . You know, a doctrine!"

"A doctrine? What for? We're happy here, admit it. We're happy because the air smells of snow and spring. Because the sun's been warming the planks, because . . . Yes, because we're together. Do the others need a doctrine to come down here to the shore and look at the fields beyond the Volga. And watch that bird flying from one branch to another in the willows?"

I would have preferred to hear a political or moral argument, a theoretical challenge, but Vika's words expressed a visible and concrete truth, difficult to contradict. The sky, the snow, the noisy trickle of the waters beneath the thick ice floes. To cover up my confusion I exaggerated the intensity of our disagreement.

"Oh, if it was only as simple as that! Of course they could come here, look at the river, breathe the good air. But they have to work! You forget that we're talking about the working class . . ."

She did not reply at once, remained still for a moment, her eyes blinking gently in the flood of sunlight. Then, in a dry, impersonal voice she asked me, "This working class, do you know what they make at that factory?"

"I don't know. Fertilizers, maybe. Or ceramic stuff . . ."

"Yes, fertilizers . . . Very explosive ones. The factory supplies chemical products to other concerns that make the charges for shells and bombs. Don't repeat that to anyone or you'll be in trouble."

She fell silent, then added in a voice that was calm once more: "This future you talk about is wonderful but too complicated. It's as if before they can come and look at the river, people have to make reinforced concrete terraces. What's the point? This old jetty's enough for us. What needs to be explained to other people is the only true doctrine. It's very simple. It all comes down to the fact . . . of loving one another."

We returned more slowly than usual. Every step, every glance now had a new meaning for me, the reflection of a world transfigured by this "fact of loving one another."

Two or three times when leaving the village, I had chanced to come across my friend's mother, a thin, short woman, her face hollow with weariness. She was called Elsa. We exchanged a few words, she invited me to come on a Saturday or Sunday to take a meal with them . . . In one of the rooms in the house I had seen a picture of Vika's father. He was, according to what she had told me one day, "absent for professional reasons." I had not sought to learn more about this: at the orphanage all my comrades had fathers who were busy sailing around the world, or they turned out to have been pilots killed in action, outnumbered in dogfights against our country's countless enemies. To cast doubt on any of this would have been cruel, faith in it made it possible not to lose all hope. Respect for these innocent lies was, for all of us, an inviolable pact.

A time came when it seemed as if my friend's mother was returning home earlier and earlier. The notion that she might have wanted to keep an eye on us did not even cross my mind, so natural was the trust that bound us together. There was, in fact, a commonplace explanation for this change in her routine. We were in March, the days were very quickly getting longer, and, as I used to leave at sunset, this time was shifting.

One evening, leaving the village, I noticed Elsa's figure walking beside the factory wall. She seemed to be waving a hand in greeting or even beckoning me to follow her. In the dusk it was hard to see and I was on the point of going my way, paying no attention to her gesture. However, an uneasy curiosity impelled me toward her.

I quickly realized that Elsa had not seen me, her summons had merely been the action of readjusting a canvas bag she carried on her shoulder. As if drawn along in a dream, I walked on beside that interminable wall . . . It was already fairly dark when the woman I was following disappeared. A minute later I reached the corner, followed around it, and involuntarily took several steps backward . . .

A battle was in progress, at once clumsy and ferocious. A crowd of women were pressed up against a plywood partition covering a passage that linked one of the factory exits to the platform beside a railroad track. This long chamber shook beneath the tramp of an invisible host leaving the building and plunging into freight wagons coupled to an engine. The women were thrusting one another aside, using their elbows, weaving their way toward the plywood screen so as to end up in front of a gap two feet wide through which the faces of men walking along the passage could be glimpsed. The violence of the struggle was unthinking, they were unaware of the blows they received or struck. The air seemed to be riven with cries held in check by fear, but which, on account of this restraint, rang out even more savagely. It was mainly men's names that went flying through the narrow opening toward the column on the move. "Sergei!" "Sasha!" "Kolya!" From time to time, a lean face appeared, a husband managed to stop opposite the gap for a few seconds. If his wife spotted him she endeavored to hand him a package, which he seized before melting into the human flow. Sometimes the package got torn, a hunk of bread and packets of tea could be seen falling in the dirty snow . . . Some names caused the appearance of a person no one was waiting for, the women would regard him with scorn and begin shouting out a surname as well. Elsa reached the opening, yelled a name in a desperate voice that froze me, and held out her canvas bag to a hand that came through the gap. A violent jolt shoved the hand back and the gap was blocked by a uniform greatcoat. The bag fell, Elsa bent down to pick it up. By the railroad track two armed guards could be seen approaching . . .

I ran along beside the wall with a very real sense of no longer existing, no longer being capable of formulating the slightest thought. I was empty, bereft of all I believed I knew, all I hoped for, dreamed of . . . Back at the orphanage it felt as though my comrades were speaking a foreign language, or rather a language whose words I knew but whose meaning I no longer understood.

The next day I had to join another paramilitary exercise, the final round, in fact, of that set of competitions during which I had captured Vika. I took part in it absentmindedly, allowing myself to be swept along in the assaults, scaling the ice ramparts as if on the brink of sleep. Even the final hand-to-hand battle, in which the two armies confronted one another, could not rouse me from my stupor. I ended up finding myself face-to-face with a youth stationed on the fortification of a defended position, who was fighting gleefully, an aggressive grimace on his lips. He noticed at once that I was not in a very warlike mood. His expression became tinged with scorn and he pushed me over with excessive brutality, evidently intending to topple me right down. I fell, becoming caught on a guardrail made of tree trunks and colliding with a block of ice. Coming to with a bleeding nose, I found myself sitting at the center of the melee, my left foot oddly twisted. Above the ankle, beneath the fabric of my pant leg, I noticed a curiously prominent lump. I looked up, saw the victor's laughing face, his astonishing delight at having caused harm. The pain was already welling up when, in a muted echo, this thought occurred to me, in a language incomprehensible to the others: "The only true doctrine . . . the fact of loving one another . . ."

My broken leg delayed my return to the village until the middle of May. Arriving there, I thought I must have stepped off the bus at the wrong stop. Instead of the little street leading to the river, a vast terrain, being turned over by bulldozers, extended all along the shore. No, I had not made a mistake for the factory was still there, its endless enclosing wall, the red letters on the roof, "an eternally living, creative, revolutionary doctrine" . . .

As for the village, all that was left of it was a single house, the one where an old woman lived whom we sometimes saw going to fetch water from the well. The only trace of the other houses was the wreckage of their timbers. The bulldozers were busy shifting these remains to the edge of the site. The roar of the engines, the acrid stench of their emissions, and, in particular, the pitiless, radiant sun, all this proclaimed the triumph of the life that forged ahead, with its promise of new happiness, victorious dynamism.

The waters had risen and the jetty was afloat several yards from the riverbank, like an island separated from this new life.

The other little island was that last house, which I went to in the evening after the noise of the demolition had ceased and the workers had gone home. The old woman who lived there did not wait to hear my questions. She understood at once why I had come. But what she told me added little to what I could already guess for myself.

There had been an accident at the factory a month earlier. Several workshops had been flattened in an explosion, becoming a mass grave for the prisoners who were brought in to work there from a nearby camp. No one knew the precise number of the victims but my friend's father was probably among them. Or else it was the demolition site on the riverbank that had caused Elsa and her daughter's sudden departure. In the previous year they had come to live in the village to be close to the factory where, for a few seconds, you could exchange glances with the prisoners as they passed through the chamber between the workshops and the freight wagons . . . With the village demolished, they had to move. So, after the explosion, Vika's father might simply have been transferred to another workplace. The old woman hinted at this possibility, wanting to give hope a little chance.

Stunned, I did not have the presence of mind to ask her what she herself was going to do amid this chaos of overturned earth. I went away, vaguely thanking her the way a neighbor certain of seeing her again the next day might have done. Many years later that old woman, whom I left all alone on the little front steps of her doomed house, would inspire feelings of remorse such as recur throughout our lives and for which we never receive absolution.

It also took me many years to learn how to appreciate, beyond a brief episode of adolescent affection, the luminous happiness my friend and Elsa, her mother, had so discreetly afforded me. Of course, I remembered their hospitality, the gentleness with which they had surrounded the wild young lad that I was, a being hardened by roughness and violence. As I grew older I would come to recognize more fully that the peace they succeeded in causing to reign in such a desolate place, yes, that serenity indifferent to the ugliness and coarseness of the world, was a form of resistance, perhaps more effective than the dissident whisperings I later heard in intellectual circles in Moscow or Leningrad. Those women's rebellion was not at all spectacular: keeping their little antiquated house perfectly neat and tidy, Vika's always even-tempered serenity, never revealing her pain, Tchaikovsky's *Seasons*, Elsa's silence and her smile, while still shaken by her vigil among the women fighting to exchange glances with their husbands or sons.

I had to wait longer still before truly recognizing what this humble and precious gift was that I had received from them. The country of our youth has sunk without trace, carrying away with it, as it foundered, the substance of so many lives of which no vestige remains. That girl locating the tune we loved on a long-playing record, her mother thrusting a canvas bag into a prisoner's hands, myself hobbling about in the mud on my broken leg . . . And a host of other lives, sufferings, hopes, griefs, promises. And the dream of an ideal city peopled by men and women who would no longer know hatred. And that "eternally living, creative, revolutionary doctrine," it, too, carried away by the frenzy of time.

All that remains now is the March light, the heady exhalation from the snows beneath the sun's dazzling rays, the wood of an old landing stage, its timbers warmed by a long day of sunshine. What remains is the pale patch of a dress on the front steps of a little wooden house. The gesture of a hand waving me good-bye. I walk on, drawing farther away, turning back after every five paces, and the hand is still visible in the mauve, luminous springtime dusk.

What remains is a fleeting paradise that lives on for all time, having no need of doctrines.

FIVE

Lovers on a Stormy Night

The moths flung themselves at every light source, collided with things, got scorched, fell, exhausted, regained their strength, hurtled back once more toward the white heat. In the face of this absurd obstinacy, one had to imagine a sublime sexual passion whose intensity made the risk of dying seem trifling.

Every evening during August that year we saw clouds of kamikaze insects bombarding the little lamps in the restaurants and the street-lights. And hordes of vacationers, seeking the heat of an embrace, the blindness of an affair, with a similar determination.

The awareness of being a part of this gave rise to ambiguous feelings in us: the joy of belonging to a bronzed, carefree tribe, hungry for love, and at the same time the disappointment of being just one more couple, a holiday romance, ephemeral and feverish, among so many others in that beach resort on the Black Sea . . .

This disagreeable feeling that we were imitating all the others was added to by our dependence on pleasure, like that induced by drugs. We had to increase the dosage, step up the frequency of our bouts of lovemaking. And our bodies would give way, exhausted, like those of the moths intoxicated with light. And every night we would be pained by this growing realization of a trite and bitter truth: pleasure only aims at itself, being a marvelous end in itself. A repetitive loop, heady, exhausting, delicious, perfumed with the scent of tanned and salty skin, molded by muscles made firm in lengthy daily swims, spiced with hot dishes and thick wine that tastes of walnuts, a panting flight toward the climax and a spiraling down into the abyss of bed linen saturated with sea spray, beneath a star hanging low among the branches of a pomegranate tree. An intoxicating cul-de-sac.

My companion during that August proved to be more aware than I of this circular dead end. Every night she watched the moths struggling against the suicidal impulse of their aerobatics . . . She was an Abkhazian, studying in Moscow and hoping, during her holidays, to experience an adventure essential to the life of a young woman of her origins: to free herself from the moral constraints of her Caucasian homeland, to love without falling in love. Yes, to be a moth fluttering amid a stream of light particles but without burning her wings. She had a name to match the best romantic scenario: Leonora . . .

Within a few days this project was accomplished: we met, free, passionate, each eager to offer the other the most attractive image of a physical relationship, to act out a fine drama of love. Our bodies performed superbly, the decor of mountains sloping down to the sea added a cinematic luster to every word, every kiss. We clasped one another with the energy of athletes, with a fierce yearning for perfection, just as if our every move were being projected onto an ever-changing screen of beautiful sunsets.

At that age one is loath to accept the brevity of pleasure. Still less, the blunting, the anodyne routine of it, ever more unsurprising, insipid. At the end of two weeks, our original thirst quenched, we had forebodings of a suffocating and vaguely matrimonial coziness.

All young lovers travel this road and all, in their alarm, have only one solution: to put pressure on the limits our poor human bodies impose on us. We doubled the violence of our embraces, seeking now the complicity of the sea at night, now the solitude of waterfalls in the forest. Following the consummation of our ecstasy, the waves would nonchalantly hurl back our entwined bodies onto the chill pebbles, turning us into gasping shipwreck victims. After lovemaking buoyed up by the sea, our walk over the stony beach to retrieve our clothes became torture. We hobbled blindly along in the darkness, groaning and limping, exiled from a paradise we believed in less and less. Or we would sally forth on a cool, misty morning for an amorous expedition upon a wooded hillside, only for it to conclude with a return in full sunlight, under the blaze of a pitiless sky, down a road where the molten asphalt was frankly reminiscent of hell.

One evening, as we emerged from the sea, we surprised another couple making love in the water. They located their clothes easily: the boy had a diver's electric flashlight fastened to his waist . . . We had the strength to find this amusing.

At the end of the third week there was a day of rain, a dark sea, yes, black, to match its name, with the laughing sob of the seagulls, a prelude to the end of the vacation. We wandered in a park, went down to the beach, picturing our nocturnal swims with a shiver, then returned to the center of town. Everything we had lived through since we met was brimming with happiness and the scenario we had written with our bodies was a palpable success. Yet we could not manage to conceal from one another a feeling of frustration. Our affair was like one of those concertinas of holiday postcards displayed under the noses of tourists. It led to nothing beyond sun-soaked clichés.

In short, it did not lead to love. That day, without admitting it, we sensed what we lacked.

Not having the courage to recognize this, we started looking for someone to blame. And the villain was very quickly unmasked!

The obstacle to our love was right there in front of us, depicted on a vast billboard that ornamented the train station's facade. An imposing face, an authoritarian gaze beneath bushy eyebrows. A fine man, in short, with a slightly receding hairline and a solid chin, sporting four gold stars on his black jacket . . .

Today his name could serve as a marker for the generations: those who have grown up since the fall of the Berlin Wall will not even remember a certain Brezhnev, images of whom once decorated one-sixth of the globe. And even in this seaside town he was everywhere to be seen: alongside roads, on the walls of holiday homes, at the central point in the big park where all the pathways met . . . Forgotten nowadays, this old potentate then presided over the destinies of a vast empire, governing the lives of hundreds of millions of people, unleashing wars at all four corners of the earth. A man whose slightest frown would cause barrels of ink to flow in newspapers across the planet . . .

Lifting our umbrella a little, we met his gaze and sighed, recognizing with resignation: yes, he was the guilty one. And, beyond him, the regime that held sway in our country and of which he was the deified incarnation.

What did those lovers pacing up and down in the driving rain need? Not much, in the end. The chance to rent a hotel room and create a little summer vacation love nest where they could feel at home. But in that era hotels were few in number and imposed identity checks more rigorously than the police. If an unmarried couple had dared to present themselves at the reception desk, they would have been suspected of madness.

The status of free lovers was on a par with that of vagabonds, thieves, dissidents. Which was not mistaken: love is in essence subversive. Totalitarianism, even in the mild form our generation knew, dreaded the spectacle of two beings embracing and escaping its control. It was less the prudishness of a moral order than the nervous tic of a secret police, refusing to admit that a tiny part of existence can lay claim to its personal mystery. A hotel room became a dangerous place: the laws of the totalitarian world were flouted there by the pleasure two people gave one another, with scant regard for the decisions of the latest Party Congress.

In these circumstances there was only one means of finding accommodation: the "private sector," as this relic of bourgeois life was then called. Little houses into which the owners struggled to cram an extravagant number of vacationers. Every room, every nook and cranny, the tiniest shed, was packed with beds in which families and couples, as well as people on their own who had come to the seaside to relieve their loneliness, all slept in a tribal lack of privacy. Inviting a person into such a wigwam was not, in principle, impossible. But to avoid the righteous anger of respectable mothers, the carnal act had to proceed at the slow tempo of those silent gyrations cosmonauts perform in orbit. At the first creak of the bed, the lovers would freeze, waiting for the neighboring snores to resume their rhythm. To put it mildly, the ponderous nature of this Kama Sutra did not go hand in hand with the full flowering of sexuality. We had dared to try it once, Leonora and I. We never repeated the experience. Hence our choices of the sea and the forest and a return every night to our respective vacation accommodations.

Hence, too, this wandering on a rainy day and our gloomy sarcasm at the sight of the portrait decorating the station front. And this joke I told my companion to cheer her up: "Have you heard? Brezhnev's just had an operation!" "Really? What's wrong with him?" "They're trying to enlarge his rib cage so they can hang another gold star on his chest . . ." With mirthless laughter we repeated what all the youth of our country used to boldly proclaim, sotto voce. The old men in the Kremlin are sabotaging our love lives. They won't let us travel freely, or read what young people in the West read, or listen to the music they listen to. ("Or drink double whiskeys in a bar on Sunset Boulevard," some wits would add, "before driving off in our convertibles.")

The days when I used to dream of that ideal city in a fraternal society were now very remote . . .

We would never have admitted that these recriminations allowed us to forget the brevity of our pleasure, the routine sameness waiting to ambush our amorous passion, and also, quite simply, the tedium of the carnal habit, a bitter reality for which not even the most democratic regime had so far found a remedy.

This dismal day would by now be quite forgotten if, as the evening approached, we had not decided to take refuge in a cinema. We felt it would have been too infuriating simply to part in the rain, going off to sleep in our respective "private sectors." We saw a poster, and the title of the film seemed to contain a comic hyperbole in response to our anti-Soviet sulks and pro-Western lamentations: *A Thousand Billion Dollars.* Yes, double whiskeys, convertibles, the lot. We hurried to the box office.

We were completely mistaken. Not as regards the quality of the film, a good action picture with talented actors, but the subject. Our fantasy Western world did not emerge unscathed: assaults on its famous freedom of expression, the press under the yoke of big capital, journalists of integrity under pressure . . . That was why this French film had achieved clearance from the Soviet censorship! Better than any kind of propaganda coming from the Kremlin, the plot exposed the hypocrisy of bourgeois society.

Despite the ideological implications the cinema was full. Partly because the spectators, mostly young couples, had nowhere else to go on a wet night. Besides, it was a good story. A young journalist played by Patrick Dewaere confronts a terrifying multinational, having discovered its certainly ancient but still criminal links to the Nazis. The intrepid investigator is threatened, hunted down, escapes a hired killer, and then, when he is almost ready to drop, goes into hiding in a small provincial town, where a local newspaper is bold enough to publish his revelations . . .

The audience responded adequately. Everyone sympathized with the journalist's plight, on the run from the baddies, waxed indignant at the machinations of the multinational, willed good to triumph over evil. These noble aspirations went hand in hand with quite a few fond hugs and kisses in the dark . . .

Suddenly I had a physical sense that the room was growing tense, gripped by a violent muscular spasm. I was aware of creaking seats and the space created by people holding their breath. Leonora, who was squeezing my hand, dug her nails into my wrist . . .

The cheer that arose was more volcanic than at any rock concert. I saw spectators leaping up, waving their arms in a feverish salute, embracing their companions in a demented frenzy. The applause drowned all the sounds coming from the screen. People were laughing, yelling, and, in the half-light, I caught several pairs of eyes glistening with tears. The rest of the film, which had almost finished, no longer mattered.

For the sequence that was being applauded had no dramatic significance and could well have been cut in the editing, so trivial was its place in the story. One evening the young journalist, in flight from his pursuers, walks into a little hotel in provincial France and asks for a room. The receptionist hands him a key, saying, "Here you are, monsieur, room fourteen" (or fifteen, or sixteen, I no longer remember). Nothing more. But it was this brief, completely anodyne exchange that threw the audience into a state of collective hysteria. For suddenly the spectators were witnessing a miracle, which apparently, somewhere in the West, was a perfectly ordinary feature of life. A man walked into a hotel and, without presenting any kind of identification, was given a room key!

The film continued, but the only image that caught anyone's eye was simply this: a pair of lovers, following hard upon the journalist's heels, also asked for a room and the sleepy night clerk handed them a key without any inquisitorial checks.

At the exit to the cinema the spectators scattered into the darkness with a strangely buoyant tread, that of children taking off from a trampoline and capering about in the air.

That evening, more effectively than all the dissidents put together, Patrick Dewaere contributed to the fall of the Berlin Wall.

During the days that followed the sun returned and up until our departure the vacation happiness unfurled its concertina of colored cards. There was joy, newfound, along with the azure of the sea's expanse; the ripening of bunches of grapes above the terraces, the vigor of our suntanned bodies. A joy too radiant not to be a little wistful. And the worst of it was that now we were familiar with that simple action; walking into a hotel and climbing up an ancient wooden staircase to a room that might have been waiting for us. A lot of the visitors to that beach resort spent the last week of August with the name of a certain French village on their minds, as well as that of the hotel there, with its sleepy night clerk taking down a key from a board bristling with little hooks.

Leonora was due to catch the evening train to Moscow, my plane was the following day. That day, from the morning onward, the weather was unbearably hot, the sky clouded over, low, suffocating. In the afternoon a dull light hung over the beaches, a storm was on the prowl, hesitant to strike. The streets were plunged into tropical darkness, like a flood of scalding ink.

The first rumbles of thunder surprised us on the road to the station. They rolled out majestically, drowning the noises of the town, the chatter of the crowd gathering alongside the platforms. Peering down from his vast portrait on the station front, Brezhnev arched an eyebrow, as if to say, "A storm? Has it been authorized by the Politburo?"

The sky turned silver and black at the same time. Sudden downpours, sporadic for the moment, drove the passengers into the little station building as though with great sweeps of a broom. We followed them, but remaining inside was torture: the stifling sultriness was loud with the yelling of children, the curses of harassed parents, and the yapping of several dogs . . . Then one lady remarked to her husband, "We've had no lunch. What we need now is some good hot borshch!" This remark was the last straw. Moving as one, we rushed outside . . .

The sky was in turmoil, laying bare the blue rifts of lightning flashes. The thunder responded, ever closer and more deafening. Our clothes were quickly wringing wet and in a movement of disarray we turned to one another, as if seeking advice. Our solitude on this empty platform in the driving rain epitomized the status of all lovers with nowhere to stay. Coming to life amid the outpourings from the heavens, the loudspeaker hissed in strangely confidential tones, as if its message only concerned this couple alone in the middle of a deluge: "All trains will be subject to a delay of two to three hours . . ." As he saw us, a railroad worker, galloping the length of the platform in great jagged leaps, shouted out, "At least!" At a loss, we took several steps, not really knowing where to go . . .

And suddenly we saw another Brezhnev.

This one was mounted on a vast billboard at right angles to the tracks, so that passengers on departing trains took the benediction of his paternal gaze with them on their journey. His face, incidentally, had suffered a serious assault: the features were streaked with two stains from overripe fruit, one beneath his left eye, the other on his chin. The infamous projectiles had doubtless been hurled from a moving train, so as to ensure an easy impunity for the terrorist. A narrow canopy above the billboard kept the rain off his face, which thus delayed the washing away of the trickles of brownish juice, probably from rotten peaches. Curiously enough, this besmirching took away the portrait's flat and foolish expression, even conferring on it an aura of profundity. This was no longer a fat apparatchik rejuvenated by a servile painter, but an older man, as Brezhnev was in reality, yes, someone who seemed to be looking down with an all-encompassing bitterness at this young couple lashed by torrential rain . . .

We took a step forward, noticing all at once that the billboard was constructed just like a sloping roof deposited on the ground. The other side, identical to the first, also bore a political message, visible to passengers departing southward: "The USSR is the bulwark of peace, democracy, and friendship between peoples!"

A thunderclap exploded so violently that we stooped instinctively and dived in beneath the roof formed by these plywood panels. We had to cross a hedge of thornbushes, stepping over lengths of wood piled there for the struts . . . This double billboard was doubtless under construction and the storm must have interrupted work on it that day. On the inside the wood still retained the dry and resinous smell from the scorching heat before the rain.

We settled down on a heap of planks, relieved to be under cover . . .

Gradually this feeling gave way to an idea both ironic and sad: yes, we finally had our little corner to ourselves, the refuge we had so much missed during our vacation. And what a refuge! On the other side of each plywood expanse we could picture Brezhnev's stained face and the slogan celebrating democracy and friendship between peoples . . . Our very own hotel room.

The silence we maintained did not weigh upon us, the scenario we had acted out for three weeks no longer held sway, everything was becoming simple and natural. Instead of a passionate embrace there was this unmoving caress of a hand upon a shoulder, a cheek pressed against fingers that smelled of the chill of the rain. The storm was moving off toward the sea, the rumbling was becoming more muted and the rain more regular, heavier.

Flashes of lightning still lit up our refuge and it was against a greenish glow that we observed the arrival of two shadowy figures in the entrance to this makeshift den. The matching crash of thunder now caught up with the lightning, and the smaller of the silhouettes shuddered while the other leaned over in a protective gesture. Our eyes, accustomed to the darkness, managed to see them fairly clearly.

They were a very elderly couple, both certainly in their eighties. More than their faces or their movements, it was their way of speaking and their demeanor that gave them away as beings who belonged to quite a different era from the one we lived in . . . They seemed not to have noticed our presence.

The man, tall and lean, wearing a broad, light-colored hat, ministered to his wife with the care one has for a child. He made her sit down on a plank covered with a sweater that he took out of his bag. Then, shaking a big umbrella, he placed it open in the entrance to the shelter, evidently to keep out drafts. His voice was tinged with firm, genial confidence.

"There you are, all's well that ends well . . . No, I feel much better now. I got a bit hot in that waiting room, that's all . . . No, it wasn't my heart, I promise you. I was just a bit breathless . . . No, those people weren't being unpleasant. Just a bit on edge, that's all. This storm, and the wind. They were frightened, you know. Otherwise, I'm sure they'd have offered us a seat . . . And it shows they think we're young. Which is encouraging. And, as for all that pushing and shoving, well, we've seen far worse, as you know . . ."

More lightning erupted, and the thunderclap drowned out his words. The blazing sky enabled us to see the old man gently clasping his wife, as if to protect her from the debris following an explosion. He began speaking again and we did not know if we should show ourselves and greet them, or simply leave them in their extreme remoteness. The more they spoke the more the distance separating them from us increased, so that our eavesdropping seemed to matter less and less.

"Remember those stations after the revolution? Now that really was some pushing and shoving! . . . What? . . . But we were. Well, we were still disguised as peasants. And then there was that day, with Red Guards all around us, when you began to speak in French . . . Now that time I really was afraid . . . Yes, I know. You were exhausted . . . And the Crimea was no beach resort in those days. Far from it . . ."

The crashing thunder interrupted their conversation again and gave us time to gather our wits: in the darkness of our den, almost within touching distance, were two survivors of tsarist Russia, two White Russians, as they used to be called, people born before the revolution, at the end of the nineteenth century, no doubt, and who, for mysterious reasons, had not emigrated to Europe, had grown old in this country, which they could not love, and at the age of more than eighty on a stormy night had wound up beneath a plywood billboard that was being shaken furiously by the squalls.

The tale continued, always in tones seeking more to reassure the old lady than to revive shared memories. The husband's voice managed it, his wife, less distressed, was joining in from time to time, to pinpoint some detail of their past. Two or three times we even heard the thin tinkle of her laughter.

The story they told could be summed up in a few sentences: the

Crimea, the ultimate bastion of the White Army, the waves of exiles who thronged there, hoping to catch a ship, cross the Black Sea, and seek refuge in Europe. This man, a young officer, fights to the end, but at the moment of defeat he does not set sail with his companions in arms because his wife is due to arrive from one day to the next. In fact, she is waiting for him at a neighboring port, convinced her husband's regiment is due to leave from there. Each of them sees one last ship preparing to depart; the people embarking on it thrust them back, or else try to drag them on board . . . They remain on the quay, they wait, see the Reds occupying the Crimea. And two months later manage to be reunited in what is already a different Russia. They change their identities, censor their conversations, try to survive, and in the end discover the remedy: in the bloody night that descends on Russia they recall luminous moments that go back to their youth. They perceive that people everywhere carry such bright glimpses of the past within themselves, but are afraid to believe in them, to share them with strangers . . . Twenty years after their wanderings in the Crimea there is another separation: the man goes off to war against Hitler, now fighting to save this new Russia he had resisted with fury in his youth . . . Over four years they meet only once, at a railroad station. The wife has become a nurse and is escorting a trainload of wounded due for evacuation toward the rear. He is in command of a regiment preparing to defend the city . . . After the victory it is once again in the middle of a vast gathering in Moscow that she comes looking for him, on his return from the front in '45. "This crowd's just like the one in the Crimea, do you remember?" he murmurs in her ear, as he clears a way for them through the demobilized troops . . . The years go by and still they have the sense that the beautiful clarity of their young days is miraculously preserved within them. It even feels as if this radiance grows more limpid, sharper, with increasing age. For the sixtieth anniversary of their marriage they travel to the Black Sea, first a week in the Crimea, then a brief stay on the coast near the Caucasus . . . On the evening of their departure a storm breaks, they escape from the general melee at the station and find themselves sheltering beneath enormous propaganda billboards. So remote from the world, so present in their own world, which they have never really left . . .

The Moscow train was announced beneath a sky already cleared of rain. We heard the station doors banging, countless footsteps rushing out onto the platforms, splashing in the pools of water. The sounds compressed within the stifling space of the station hall exploded into the open air: quarreling, children crying, rallying calls to family members, dogs barking . . .

Without giving ourselves away, we allowed the two elderly travelers to move off. We quickly lost sight of them in the crowd, but when we reached the coach Leonora was due to get into we realized it was also theirs. They approached as we were saying good-bye. Now we noticed how different they were from the rest. An ordinary couple of their age would have rushed toward the steps up to the coach with an air of panic, pushing us aside, perhaps, anxious that the train was about to depart, concerned to secure their seats . . . The old man and his companion at once appreciated that before them stood two young lovers on the brink of parting. They stopped and even drew back a little, remarking quietly that the storm was moving southward . . .

Instead of any conventional outpourings, my friend bowed her head slightly and my lips brushed her brow. This unintentionally chaste kiss seemed to us the most beautiful of all those we had exchanged that summer . . . Leonora climbed in swiftly. From afar we heard the whistle of the engine. The old man helped his wife to scramble up the high, steep steps and unhurriedly mounted them in his turn, content, it appeared, to feel the train already moving under his feet. I kept my eyes fixed on his tall, straight old soldier's figure and his wife's face, her eyes open wide, gazing at the line of mountains outlined by the moon's dull gold . . .

Walking away, I extracted a tiny ball of damp paper from my pocket; it was the scrap on which Leonora had written her address. I reflected that my own must have become just as illegible in her jeans pocket. The loss did not distress me. A much more intense bond united us, a memory that made it unimportant whether we saw one another

again. I did not know how to express this conviction, I simply saw the
glow of it, calm, constant, detached, unconnected with the flight of
the years. And it has not faded since.

Ten years later the dream Patrick Dewaere had given rise to among the
vacationers on the Black Sea that summer was realized. The Berlin Wall
fell and hotels sprang up on the soil of the former Soviet empire like
mushrooms after rain: lovers could stay at them freely, provided they
were not poor.

Another sign of the times was the waxworks museum that opened in
Moscow, along the lines of Madame Tussauds's famous crowd of phantoms. A friend dragged me there one day, wanting to show me a character
he considered to be "staggering." The epithet was well chosen, for this
was an old man sitting in a rocking chair. An ingenious device, a system
of ropes and pulleys, was installed beside the wall. Visitors could pull
a handle and the old man wrapped in a tartan blanket would begin to
move, rocking to and fro more and more wildly but kept in place by
chocks. The sculptor had contrived to endow this old face with a mixture
of foolish satisfaction and unease. People were laughing, making rude
comments . . .

      With a strange twinge of bitterness, I recognized the character. It
was Brezhnev. Not the face-lifted apparatchik of the official portraits
but a human ruin, wrapped in a blanket, lurking in his quarters at the
Kremlin, nervously waiting for the end.

      My friend was exultant.

      "Would you believe it? What a symbol! Imagine this little number
ten years ago. What am I saying? . . . Even five years ago! They'd have
put us all behind bars just for doing a drawing of this old wreck! And
to think that a dummy like this could have blighted our best years, the
whole of our youth, in fact! Wait, I'm going to pull this. Look at him
rocking. Isn't that a riot! Go on. You take a turn. It'd be good to tip him
right over . . ."

He indicated the handle. I hesitated, then refused, on the pretext that I wanted to move on to other figures from history. We walked on through the galleries, encountering the glassy stares of dictators, stars, the founders of empires . . .

Then the memory returned to me of that old couple under a stormy sky in a little beach resort on the Black Sea. The White Army veteran and his wife. Who might hold the old man in his rocking chair in more contempt than these two survivors of the Russia of long ago? Who more than they had a right to redress on the part of History? And yet I was absolutely certain that they would never have grasped the avenging handle. For there was no hatred in their hearts. Just the glow from those moments of past time the man talked about so as to restore his companion's composure during that stormy night. "Do you remember the day," he had said, as they sheltered under that den made out of billboards, "when I found you again in the Crimea? It was winter. An ice-cold day, brilliant sunshine. And we were starving . . . Then you picked two bunches of grapes in an abandoned vineyard, the last of them, ones that had escaped both birds and men. They were shriveled raisins but divinely sweet. Like nuggets of light. We ate them and walked on again . . ."

On those occasions, all too rare, alas, when I come across two ancient beings as unmistakably filled with tenderness, I always picture their lives as a long journey on a brilliantly limpid, sunny day, each with a golden bunch of grapes in their hands.

SIX

A Gift from God

Trapeze artists must feel as supple as this, bounding from one flight to the next. Their movements slot into one another, airily natural, sculpting space with the broad swing of their bodies.

This morning we fly across the town like that.

Waking late, a panic-stricken glance at the watch, actions driven by a backward countdown from a bus timetable. The thrill of seeing how, as hardened night owls, after three hours' sleep we contrive to make up for lost time. Acrobats and jugglers simultaneously, squeezing into the narrow space of the shower, before our laughing looks meet in the mirror above the washbasin, frenzied toothbrushes, the smell of coffee wafted over by a draft, a hunk of bread, a slice of cheese swallowed without sitting down, a sudden whirlwind of clothes and then a woman's body, erect, as if after a gymnast's leap, mounting onto high heels and straightening up, five inches taller.

We run along the drowsy streets, cutting diagonally over crossroads. No cars in this little town, a Sunday morning, the pigeons move aside lazily as we pass. As we reach the bus station, a shelter with dusty glass windows, we can see a coach embarking on its turning circle, about to depart. Board her now, my hearties! The driver brakes, indulgent as people are for a couple of lovers. We kiss and my girlfriend climbs in quickly. The passengers bite back their routine grumbling and smile at this young woman swaying on her heels, as she makes her way along the bus in a tornado of perfume. The dull gray of one of the windows right at the back is lit up by an animated look and the flick of a mane of fair hair tossed over her shoulder. And already the red spot of the bus is receding, vanishing into the gray air of this spring morning.

Her departure leaves me with a solitude it is easy to bear (we shall meet again this evening) but also this vague sense of loss: a body that gave itself to me last night will shortly be plunged into the crowds of a big city, the noisy bustle of the Nevsky Prospekt, inviting male curiosity.

Even more than the bittersweet interrupted continuity of our brief separation, however, what intoxicates me is the floating lightness of it, the weightlessness of a misty May morning, the softly tinted transparency of the first, still pale, foliage. I feel as if I could fly over it. Yes, like a trapeze artist.

. . . When love affairs no longer lay claim to the uniqueness of a grand passion, the poisoned chalice they have to offer is a delicious non-chalance about our feelings. At this stage in our youth we are still too carefree to realize this constitutes agnosticism. What we relish, above all, is the emotional and physical ease with which relationships are formed, flower, give way to the next. Instead of the solemn amatory monotheism of adolescence, with its ecstatic organ music, we are relieved to discover the aimless, multiple idolatry of inconstancy. We learn to whistle Bach . . .

This was even truer for those of us who, during the twilight of the messianic Soviet project, wanted to forget the creaking solemnity of its theatrical scenery. My impassioned quest for the fraternal society had long since been set aside along with the dusty relics of other childish dreams. We had got the message: all that mattered was to enjoy life and, in order to avoid getting caught up in the grim rituals of a petrified ideology, we had to skip, airborne as an acrobat on his tightrope, from one love affair to another, from one fleeting pleasure to the next . . .

The red glow of the bus disappears around the corner and I prepare to walk home, still intoxicated with a love unencumbered by the weight of passion.

And it is almost at random, with an absentminded glance, that I notice a contorted figure slipping through the terminal. My recall is instant: I know that young man. For years I have contrived to avoid him . . .

I could ignore him again on this occasion. He has certainly seen me: he just had time to spot the two of us together, our quick kiss, my girlfriend's lithe dash to board the bus. He also knows I have noticed his presence and am hesitating over greeting him. I am certain he will not do so first, out of shyness and a remnant of pride . . . Three-quarters turned away from him, I can let him go on his way without feeling too much remorse.

What impels me toward him is a combination of generosity and conceit: true, I genuinely feel sorry for this fellow, but hailing him is also a way of relishing my luck in being a brilliant lover, a lethargic dandy, on a high after a long night of love . . .

I swing around and yell, with exaggerated surprise, "Hey, Zhorka! So, don't we recognize old friends anymore?"

If men had hearts of steel, Zhorka would have told me to get lost, mentioning all the times I had avoided him, all the encounters missed when I walked past without stopping, looking the other way as he went on sweeping outside the furniture factory where he worked. On such occasions he must have followed me with his eyes for a long time, telling himself by way of consolation that perhaps I had not recognized him . . .

He turns and his disfigured face registers an innocent delight. To be greeted in the street by a friend like this is too rare an event for him to allow himself to spoil it with any rancor. The people waiting at the

bus stop watch us going up to one another, and deep down inside me
a brief, selfish regret wells up. "I shouldn't have done this . . . It's too
much effort!"

His story is a simple, brutal, and unbearably stupid one. He was born
in the decade following that of the war. Our generation: the children
who came into the world ten, eleven, or twelve years after the end of
the fighting. The distance that separated us from the war then seemed
to us immense. As time passed, I would come to realize that those ten
years were nothing; the war was still on the prowl, in the mutilated
bodies of soldiers, in the danger of abandoned ammunition, which we
often unearthed in our games on former battlefields . . . One day there
was this huge shell we found in a trench. We had dragged it out to deal
with it in our usual way: a bonfire, with this steel firecracker slowly heat-
ing before exploding and shaking the earth beneath our bodies as we
lay in wait in a nearby copse. That night there was an icy mist, the fire
was slow to catch, what was needed was for someone to get close to it
and toss in some dry bark. None of us was foolhardy enough to do so;
the shell had been cooking for a long time. Then Zhorka got up, went
down into the trench, poked the fire, even had time to take several steps
away from it . . . The noise deafened us and it was in the muffled silence
caused by the explosion that a perfectly still image appeared: a small
human figure poised amid the clods of earth hurled skyward . . . Then
life began to move again but at what seemed like a sleepy tempo. The
dust fell to the ground, we were walking toward the trench as if against
the current of time, and I saw a trickle of blood flowing very gently
down the trunk of a young tree stripped of its bark by the shrapnel . . .
After several operations our comrade became the way we knew him now,
a cripple whose face would remain partly calloused by the fire, a young
hunchback confronting the world with the mournful stare of his right
eye and a terrifying stare from his glass left eye. He also retained his
diminutive name, "Zhorka," which kept him locked forever into that

spring evening when his childhood ended, not to launch him out into adolescence but thrusting him aside onto the verges of life in a dull continuation, without savor, where the transition from one age to the next made no difference.

"Where are you off to, then?"

I put on a hearty voice, as people do when trying to cover up their embarrassment at addressing a social outcast.

"Oh . . . to the station. You see, I'm going to pick morels . . ."

His voice is also too loud for this humdrum exchange. The unblemished side of his face turns a little pink. For a moment he has ceased to be any different from other people, someone has greeted him in the street, he has stopped and is talking quite naturally to an old chum.

"Ah, morels, I see. So, are you very keen on them?"

"No, the fact is . . . I sell them. That sometimes makes me an extra ten rubles a month . . ."

This confidence embarrasses him, he looks down, mutters, "Well, anyway. Good to see you. I'd better go and get my train. I'll see you around . . ."

He gives me his hand, walks away. And he is palpably making a superhuman muscular effort not to reveal his limping gait. The thick shoe on his right foot drags against the asphalt but his shoulders are straight, from a distance his disability would not be noticed . . .

I catch up with him at the entrance to the train station.

"Listen, I'm coming with you! It's ages since I went mushroom picking. And, as for morels, I wouldn't begin to know where they grow . . ."

He tries to reply but he has a lump in his throat, he merely nods his head in agreement and shows me his basket, emitting a grunt, both happy and embarrassed. We settle into a little local train in which the wooden seats are occupied by town dwellers who are off this Sunday to dig their vegetable plots in the nearby countryside.

I am intoxicated by my role as a male juvenile lead sharing a little of his good fortune with a pariah. I talk with vibrant energy so that everyone can hear us, so that this little hunchback, crammed in opposite me, should enjoy half an hour of illusion and oblivion. I manage to hit a chatty and theatrically natural note that turns our talk into an everyday conversation between two friends of the same age. I refer to our school-day memories, mention several girls' names.

"Do you remember Kira, the one we called Red Riding Hood, who used to dance like a madwoman? And her friend Svetka? You drew a picture of her on the blackboard. Do you remember?"

This is ancient history, from before the explosion. I am talking about our radiant childhood, laughing, joking, almost managing to erase the gulf between his two lives. And with a delight that is becoming less and less selfish, I notice our neighbors are gradually letting themselves be hypnotized by the gaiety of our chat. I am no longer intercepting alarmed or pitying glances like those directed at my friend during our first minutes of travel. People are no longer paying him any attention, they read their newspapers, yawn, address one another absentmindedly, look out the window. Zhorka's voice is relaxed now and only a particular attentiveness could detect the hidden tension, like the stage fright behind the smile of a young singer blinded by theatrical lighting.

There are two kinds of disabled people: those who make much of their problem, proclaim their handicap noisily, extorting obligatory compassion from us, and the self-effacing ones, who bear their cross in silence but who, if we come upon them privately, allow us to sense the aura of a constrained but rich existence, one that makes the lives of those of us in good health seem strangely impoverished.

From habit long since instinctive, Zhorka has sat down in a corner, so the disfigured half of his face remains hidden from passengers walking through the coach. He tilts his head toward his shoulder so that only his good eye can be seen. His injured foot with its enormous shoe is tucked under the seat. An unobservant glance would simply see a young man, a little on the squat side, chatting happily with a comrade.

"That drawing of Svetka? Yes, I remember. First the teacher made me erase it in front of the class. Then she gave me two hours' detention. And she said I was 'Picasso in his pink period.' It's true. I was blushing with shame!"

We laugh and I am no longer searching his face for old scars.

Gradually the amateur gardeners leave the train, the grid of fields gives way to forest. We get off at a stop where the dirt platform makes it look like a simple woodland clearing. The sun is already high, the air is as hot as in July, but in the thickets there is a chill that pricks our breathing with an icy bitterness.

Deep in the shadiest areas the last snowdrifts still lurk in hollows. The noise of the train dies away, we plunge into the mystery of this forest, barely tinged with green and therefore more silent than in summer, when the leaves on the trees all converse in their own languages. Zhorka knows the place well and I allow myself to be led, with the pleasant, childlike acceptance one feels in the company of a forest guide. We climb onto a mound covered in heather, skirt a damp valley, walk beside a little stream in which every stone, caught in a sunbeam, looks like a jewel. At first I try to continue our conversation but the words quickly run out, we no longer have any need to act like old school friends with a lot to say. Zhorka is in his element, the shade of the thickets, the last traces of snow rustling underfoot, silence. From time to time he crouches, carefully moves dead leaves aside, and unhurriedly cuts the stem of a morel. He lets me smell his first catch: a scent that strangely reminds me of a winter's evening, a forgotten joy . . . I try to copy him, rummaging in the layer of pine needles, lifting fallen branches, but I find nothing. Strolling aimlessly through this forest on the brink of summer is happiness enough for me. The main thing is not to lose sight of Zhorka's limping figure, not to trample on the tiny, pale flowers growing up through the rotting leaves here and there, not to breach the secret understanding that links me to this good fellow vanishing and reappearing among the trees.

The thoughts we share in our silent wanderings are vivid. I bring to mind our childhood not long after the war and the horrors we escaped. Our generation was able to turn the page, thrusting on toward the future in the round dance of youthful love affairs. Zhorka, for his part, did not have our luck. The past, like a snowdrift dormant in the undergrowth, made him stumble, he fell, was caught, dragged down by an era when dying was so commonplace. The injustice that struck him is repellent, unacceptable, and yet stupidly ordinary, like all the wretched accidents in our lives. If only he had waited thirty seconds longer, lying beside his comrades, the shell would have exploded and . . .

Ah, these "if onlys"! What devil or stroke of fate impelled him to stand up that day, go down to the fire, and stir the embers? I could have held him back by grabbing his sleeve or tripping him up, or gone myself to the shell baking in the fire. In the latter case it would now have been me hobbling along, disfigured, through these springtime thickets . . .

He must have turned such ideas over in his head a thousand times since that day. Asking himself: "Why me? What am I being punished for?" The years passed and he grew accustomed to putting up with himself as he now was, the questions remained unanswered.

I also bring to mind that moment frozen in time: a boy's body suspended amid a cascade of earth thrown up by the explosion. A static liftoff that our terrified eyes cut out and photographed for all time. The moment when fate must have pondered whether it would not be better to kill this child rather than granting him life as a cripple. For Zhorka this toss-up was to become a haunting theme that only suicide could have laid to rest. Was it a step he ever considered?

Is he considering it now, as he walks along slowly here in this forest, crouching, caressing the layer of dead leaves? At intervals he turns, smiles at me, always with his head tilted on one side. What can he expect from this life? A woman's gentleness, a love affair? Surely not. It is as if his body had been crushed with particular care so as to eliminate the least chance of such an encounter, a tender relationship. So what remains for him? He will sell these morels, buy a bottle of cheap wine, and, overcome with drink, dream. But of what? Of whom?

The image of Zhorka alone, drunk, is so intolerable to me that I fall back on a glimmer of hope, a happy outcome such as we always con-

jure up for social outcasts: this disabled man and a young woman, herself
a cripple, a little human warmth, a soul mate who might . . .

I catch myself hoping for this with rare fervor, as if it were a wish
I would like to see granted whatever the cost. All at once I feel bereft
of my acrobat-lover's self-assurance, prepared to renounce some part of
my own happiness, so that their humble happiness might be possible. I
could, for example, accept an end to my own affair, a period of loneliness, separation from the woman I had accompanied to the bus station
that morning . . .

The feeling is sincere, almost a prayer, it makes me realize that
something essential is lacking from the freewheeling frivolity of my life.

I snap out of it and shake off these solemn thoughts, picture my
girlfriend's return this evening, being reunited with her, the carefree
hunger of desire, a night spent making love, laughing, delighting in jug-
gling with words, caresses, plans for a summer that will soon be here . . .
The prospect of this takes me further still from the purpose of our
mushroom hunt, I smile: my setting off at the drop of a hat to meander
through a damp wood in the company of a hunchback who looks like a
character from a fairy tale is all of a piece with my casual lifestyle. The
real charm of it, indeed, is being able to flit like a butterfly from one
possibility to another, each one a little anarchic, a little ludicrous. I walk
on, relax, no longer thinking about Zhorka . . .

I locate him from the snapping of a branch at the edge of an aspen
spinney. His lame leg has caught on a root. Fallen to his knees, he gets
up with tangled clumsiness. I am distressed to see how awkward his disability makes him: it costs him an effort, pushing against the ground
with both hands, to stand up . . .

"We won't go any farther," he tells me, showing me a field beyond
which the blue glow of a fine ancient forest can be seen, with tempt-
ingly majestic trees. "Those fields were mined during the war. There's no
knowing what might still be hidden there . . ."

His voice is dull, marked by anger held in check, which quickly
exhausts itself in weariness.

"There are so many of those damned things still buried . . ."

"But what about your morels? You've not found many, have you?"

I laugh to distract him from the vision of that field where death lurks.

He shakes his basket gently, the mushrooms in it are covered by fern fronds, it is only half full.

"It's OK. I've picked ten. That'll pay for my ticket. That'll do . . ."

He gives me his little oblique smile and we set out on the return journey.

I follow in Zhorka's footsteps and our jaunt seems to me even more pointless than before. He had gone out to earn a bit of money, with which, no doubt, to buy himself some cheap alcohol, his philter for love and dreams. But he has only gathered enough to pay for the journey. Poor fellow! I try to turn my thoughts away from this short figure, limping along in front of me; I no longer want to expose myself to the heartbreaking stupidity of his tormented life.

The train we catch is packed, we have to travel standing up, surrounded by other passengers. Zhorka lowers his head, like an animal at bay, and can no longer hide the scars on his face from public gaze. People climb on board, hot after a long afternoon of gardening, their faces red from the sun, their voices raw with thirst. They jostle us unceremoniously; some of them notice Zhorka's disfigurements and move away, not troubling to hide their embarrassment or disgust. In the end he presses a hand to his brow and remains motionless, with the gesture of a person trying to remember something extremely important. His eyes are closed.

On arrival, we take a few steps together, suddenly aware that the trip is over and we are bound to separate now, perhaps for many years, as before this encounter, diverging into lives too different for our paths often to cross. We stop at a road junction, which is indeed the parting of our ways.

"So, it was great to see you again, Zhorka! We really must . . ."

My tone is almost natural, I manage to convince myself that tomorrow or the next day, who knows, we are going to meet again, renew the ties of our boyhood friendship of long ago . . . Zhorka nods, his head tilted on one side, then, as I am preparing to say good-bye and make myself scarce, he raises his basket a little, parting the fern fronds that protect his morels . . .

And he lifts out a round, compact little bouquet made up of a multitude of white flowers, snowdrops, like the ones I saw in the forest.

"Take them," he says. "You could give them to . . . to someone. But wrap something around the stalks, or the heat of your hand will wither them. Look, here's a bit of newspaper . . . Yes, I was glad to see you, too . . . Well, good luck."

He is already walking away without looking back, moving as fast as his legs will allow. I am tempted to go after him, to thank him . . . But I am afraid of meeting his gaze again. As he gave me the bouquet he stared at me and I believed both his eyes were equally alive, so intense did the fluid sparkle seem to me that flashed out briefly from beneath his eyelids.

I go home walking slowly, mentally repeating his words: "You could give them to . . . to someone." This someone is my girlfriend, whom he saw climbing into the bus this morning. He saw our lovers' embrace, our kiss . . . And so while walking in the forest he must have been thinking about that young woman, about her beauty, about the love between us. It made him forget his morels and pick mainly flowers, dreaming of the moment when she would come back and find them in the evening.

At home, I put the bouquet in a short vase and the flowers revive, forming a superb, snowy cluster. Their corollas are faintly tinged with blue, like the incrustations of that pale sky that were reflected in the puddles of melted snow in among the trees. I picture Zhorka, alone in his room, thinking about my girlfriend's surprise when she sees the flowers and asks me, "Goodness, where do these marvelous things come from?" And I shall reply, "An old school friend picked these snowdrops for you . . ." And so he will feature in the thoughts of a young woman in love, whose affection will extend to him a very little bit through the reflection of the bouquet in her big, beautifully made-up eyes . . . Yes, he must be living that dream now.

My friend reaches me late, arriving on one of the last buses from Leningrad. She comes in, kisses me, sees the bouquet. And asks no questions. She quite simply leans forward, buries her face in the subtly scented halo of flowers, closes her eyes. And when she stands up, her eyes are misty with tears. "They smell of winter," she says. "We met in December, didn't we . . ."

That night there is an unaccustomed gentleness in the way we make love, as if we had found one another again after a very long separation, having suffered greatly and grown old.

A quarter of a century later a memory returns to me like something out of a run-of-the-mill psychological novel: during that day she spent in Leningrad, my friend had met a man, her future husband. The rest of our love affair has now faded into a hazy glimmering of juvenile frivolity, insouciance, futile sentimentality. With an effort of memory I could reconstruct snatches of jealousy, faint echoes of remarks exchanged at the time we broke up, two or three physical recollections that have survived erasure. Nothing else. Nothing.

But far removed from this slipping away of phantoms, a slow dusk in May persists. The half-light of a room, the bluish glow of a bouquet in a vase. A woman goes up to it, plunges her face into the chill of the flowers, stands up again dreamily, her eyes brimming with a sadness that I do not yet understand. And a night of love persists in which every gesture seems endowed with a new meaning, a fervent tenderness. A night in which we feel very frail, already condemned by time. And in that night utterly immortal.

When speaking of Zhorka's death, those of my friends who knew him always refer to a fatal accident that occurred when he was twenty-six. So, a few months after we went out to pick morels. An accident . . .

That day, in October, Zhorka took the same little train, followed the same footpaths, made his way through the forest, this time glowing with golden foliage. He was not carrying a basket, nor a knife for cutting mushrooms. At the edge of a broad field strewn with russet leaves he stopped for a moment, took a deep breath, then walked straight ahead . . . There were two explosions: the first mine killed him; the second was set off by the detonation of the first. A hunter who was in the area raised the alarm.

For a long time I felt great and inevitable pity for Zhorka, an almost obligatory sympathy. Not anymore. For in the end I grasped that he had risen far above our human games, our grudges, regrets, remorse. I bring to mind his limping figure, swiftly retreating, leaving me with a bouquet in my hands. He gives me the flowers, walks away, and, amid the fleeting and forgetful haste of my days, his gesture opens onto the start of a life that endures, like the beauty of that woman's face made fragrant by the wintry scent of the snowdrops.

"A gift from on high!" I often say to myself, not knowing how better to express the simplicity with which this little cripple gave me perhaps the truest moment of love of all those I have ever known.

And, as if to prove the reality of this gift that he bore within him, he froze one day at the edge of a field, paused to steady his breathing and moved forward, his gaze upon the golden outline of an ancient forest far away.

At this moment his actions and thoughts were no longer addressed to us humans.

From time to time I also recall his warning regarding those first, very delicate, spring flowers, whose stems can be withered by the brutal heat of our blood.

Like the souls of the beings we love.

SEVEN

Captives in Eden

For several miles the splendor surrounding us has not varied. Foaming blossom along the boughs, the whipped cream of petals, a white wave spilling the length of an avenue of apple trees where we walk, intoxicated by their scent, which has gradually replaced the air. As if, finding ourselves on an unknown planet, we had grown used to breathing an atmosphere made up of supernatural perfumes instead of the customary combination of terrestrial gases.

After a while our heads begin to spin, it feels as if we are slowly floating along this aromatic corridor that stretches out before us to infinity.

I have never in my life seen such an immense orchard, "ten miles by fourteen," the young woman I am escorting has informed me. It is already an hour and a half since we entered this realm of blossom so that, if we keep straight on along the central avenue, it will take us another two or three hours to walk the length of this gigantic apple orchard. But, more than its extravagant dimensions, what dazzles me is its beauty. Under a powerful sun, this frothy tide washes over us, dazes us with its fragrances, sets us reeling in the dream every man cherishes, that of finding himself walking upon the clouds' curvaceous vapors . . .

There is perfect silence: not one insect, no birds, an unchanging light, the sky deep blue, the immaculate purity of the flower heads, a sweetness hangs in the air. It is paradise!

And yet we are here to demonstrate that all this is a hell. Such is the task undertaken by my friend, a journalist and a passionate dissident, determined to denounce this "model orchard" in a samizdat article as one of the absurd creations of Soviet socialism in decline.

"Look, the whole madness of the communist system is concentrated here. A monstrous orchard with a purely ideological purpose: to create the biggest plantation in the world. A triumph of collectivist agriculture! And that's not all. Whenever the old crocodiles in the Kremlin drive past from Moscow to Kiev, what they see from their limousines is a continuous spread of white. Because the trees, as you can observe, are planted close together . . ."

"It's very pretty . . ."

"Pretty! Grow up, for goodness sake! You've got a mental age of ten: and you've had it ever since we were at the orphanage . . . 'Pretty'! What you need to know, my poor friend, is that this orchard is completely unproductive. No bee wants to bust its guts flying five miles to reach the center of this crazy plantation. As a result, the flowers are not pollinated and the trees don't bear fruit. No apples will ever grow in this ideal apple orchard. It's sterile! Just like the regime we have the misfortune to live under. Now do you get it?"

I have concurred, with my head hunched between my shoulders, like a slightly stupid but eager and willing pupil. My friend has now concluded her exposition.

"Well, it may be pretty. But it's a beauty that's perfectly useless."

I felt tempted to speak up for the wonderful uselessness of beauty, but this argument suddenly seemed devoid of interest. The white ocean we were slowly immersing ourselves in made all critical judgments increasingly beside the point. Of course one could mock the Soviet obsession with size, the will to transform every detail of reality into a propaganda message. And this inevitable slide into absurdity, a tendency typical of totalitarian regimes in the throes of senility. I could hardly fail to agree with my friend's caustic comments. But the mind was quickly exhausted, as the white tide turned into an intoxication, one's gaze dilated and offered quite a different way of seeing, of understanding, of situating oneself in relation to the world.

At first my friend had wanted to photograph this example of a "Potemkin village, Soviet style," as she called it. She took several shots, realized she was defeated.

"You'd have to go to the moon to get the perspective needed for megalomania on this scale!"

She put away her camera and we began walking again, no longer venturing any commentary on the floral torrent as it swept us along in its glorious madness.

Little by little we have lost all track of time and space.

And yet the moment in history when our walk took place, back in the mideighties, was particularly significant. The old crocodiles in the Kremlin my friend had referred to were dying one after the other. A young leader, whose name was hardly known as yet, was giving rise to confused hopes. Our disillusioned compatriots had little faith in this. The existing regime seemed to be destined for a pathetic, protracted old age, encroaching on our thirst for freedom, deluging us with lies, provoking ridicule with creations as monstrous as they were absurd. Yes, this apple orchard among them.

The little breeze of change that arose that spring produced an unexpected reaction on the part of intellectuals hostile to the regime: instead of rejoicing at these first signs of the thaw, the dissidents attacked the decrepit regime more virulently than ever and, with redoubled intransigence, demanded immediate and radical liberalization. And it was notable that now everyone declared himself to be a dissident. They were not so common in the years when Shalamov was in the Kolyma gulag . . .

I did not dare mention the paradox of this tardy militancy to my companion. I was too keen for us to remain friends. First of all, because

I had known her since she was a child and was aware that, already in her teens, she was fiercely rebellious, hence her nickname at the orphanage, "Red Riding Hood": she had moved heaven and earth to get herself a scarlet knitted hat, to thumb her nose at our regulation gray headgear . . . She had also come to see me a month earlier at the military hospital where I was receiving treatment for burns sustained in a helicopter crash in Afghanistan. I was touched by her visit, being already aware that in this life ties of affection can easily be broken, particularly when one goes off to a war everybody thinks is pointless. In reality, she had not come because she carried a torch for me, nor to indulge in nostalgia for our childhood. Her aim was to publish what I had to say in her samizdat newspaper . . . But I was a poor storyteller, capable only of echoing her own views: yes, a dirty war, a moribund ideology trying to export itself and sacrificing thousands of young lives in the process . . . My friend was hoping I would talk to her about the opposition, which, according to her, must necessarily be making itself felt in the regiments. I had disappointed her there too: a soldier becomes a fairly basic creature who simply wants to survive, and for this he finds it convenient not to think too much. "So, no way of resisting?" "Yes, there is. Drink. And drugs . . ."

When I emerged from the hospital she invited me on this dissident expedition to the model apple orchard. Was she counting on having a little more time to get me to talk about my past as a soldier? Or did she simply prefer to have a man with her on this trip through remote countryside?

Now we advance in silence, through a soft, white, perfectly unmoving dream. No breath of air can penetrate the bloom-laden density of these innumerable trees, no sound: their branches awash with petals do not stir, nor do their shadows along the avenue. I know my friend is there to gather proof of the rank stupidity revealed by such an arboricultural project and yet I can feel she is increasingly disconcerted, her verdict had been reached before our excursion, but she had not foreseen this insane plantation's magnificent lack of proportion. I glance at her furtively from time to time. She walks with an uncertain tread, looking to the right, to the left, with vaguely distressed incredulity. This white avalanche in which we are drowning is extraordinarily beautiful, it cannot be denied. Beautiful to the point of ecstasy, to the point of swooning, so unbelievably beautiful that, in admiring it, one gradually forgets who one is, even forgetting that at some time one will have to abandon this hazy reverie and return to one's previous life.

What life? I read this question in my friend's wide-open eyes. And the avenue unfolds in front of us, still with the same milky brilliance, an unchanging, hypnotic, endless pathway.

At length I myself experience a slight uneasiness: ten miles by fourteen? What if my friend were mistaken and it was not fourteen miles but forty? There are no limits to folie de grandeur. To rid myself of this incipient anxiety I try to find words for all this white spilling over us. Coiners of fine phrases might speak of "bridal" or "arctic" or even "virginal" white . . . I can only smile, such expressions are so far from what we are actually breathing, seeing, and perceiving with every part of our beings.

But how, above all, to evoke the presence of this friend at my side, a little girl from the past, Kira, known as "Red Riding Hood," who has grown into a magnificent young woman with red hair, a finely chiseled face, a muscular body alive in every one of its curves? A woman who, when she came to the hospital, aroused in me hopes of bonding, affection. But who is passionately in love with another, a man involved, like her, in this business of dissidence and clandestine publications, which is all so alien to me. He is the hero of her life. I am merely an old childhood friend, she made this clear to me just as I was preparing to settle into the role of a wounded soldier with whom a woman falls in love . . .

I steal a glance at her, her eyes are open wide, her lips are moving slightly, and in her mind she must be anticipating giving an account of our expedition to the man she loves.

The glorious monotony of the avenue is suddenly interrupted; it broadens out and opens onto a circular space, the topographical center of the giant apple orchard, it seems. Another avenue forms a geometrically precise intersection with ours. We are thus at the heart of this dreamlike universe.

The middle of this round area is occupied by a ring of concrete, a very shallow basin whose edges are half covered with thick slabs of pink marble. It is a fountain under construction, or rather an abandoned one. Pipes eaten away by verdigris lie amid heaps of gravel and sand. And at the bottom of the basin a very fine trickle of water winds around. It must have been flowing there for years because its persistent current has filled a tiny pool, held in by the gravel barrier. The rains have dispersed the sand, creating a little strip of beach. Flecks of mica gleam in the crystal-clear water, along with a coin, certainly lost by a workman.

My friend does not conceal her delight. Unease at finding ourselves in an endless avenue is dissipated. This central space is a good indication that we have reached the halfway mark in our journey: another two hours' walk and we will emerge at the other end of this sterile dream.

Kira proclaims this out loud with a laugh, referring again to the absurdity of the regime she and her friends are up in arms against.

"What's really stupid is that this Soviet era won't even leave beautiful ruins behind. Just the debris of abandoned construction sites, like this ridiculous fountain . . . I know, why don't I take a dip? I'm boiling hot. And I've got my swimsuit. I was thinking of going to the pool when we get back. But I'm afraid this jaunt is going to take more time than I thought. Right, you can do what you like, but I'm getting in! I'm going to take the waters, Soviet-style . . ."

She goes in among the trees to change, reappears in a bathing suit. The arrogant contours of her body take my breath away, a body already suntanned and more bursting with femininity than I could have imagined. The water in the little pool barely reaches halfway up her calves, but this does not stop her stretching out full length in it, splashing herself with it, even, for my amusement, pretending to be really swimming . . .

The cool water renews her energy. She hoists herself up onto a pile of sand and embarks on an impassioned account of "their" struggle. Secret meetings in Moscow, Leningrad, Kiev. Manuscripts they contrive to send to the West in diplomatic bags. Long hours at night spent making microfilms that will immortalize these texts upon which the fate of humanity depends. Especially a certain text, tragically unfinished—for it is touched with genius—the novel Kira's friend has stopped writing. He is hindered by the stifling climate the regime imposes as well as the scale of his literary undertaking ("The seven decades of Soviet rule!" Kira explains to me. And in hushed tones she reveals the title, *Captives in Absurdia*) . . . The agonies of creativity are aggravated by the enforced remoteness imposed on this rebellious author.

In hushed tones, in turn, I ask sympathetically, "Is he in the gulag?"

I sense Kira's slight embarrassment.

"No, not exactly. More in exile. Thirty miles from Moscow, maybe even farther. Just picture it. Sending an artist like him among peasants, to a kolkhoz full of drunken idiots, where he has to live in a hut with a leaking roof!"

She waxes indignant without even suspecting that her words might make me jealous. In fact, I hardly exist for her. I try not to give myself away, not to show that the life she describes seems to me full of contradictions.

"And this man, your friend, that is. Does he have . . . a profession? Does he work?"

Kira flashes a scorching look at me.

"Him, work? But he's a creative artist! He's fighting the regime that frustrates his talent. That's a full-time occupation! I can see you really don't get it at all . . ."

I stammer out a conciliatory protest: "I do, I do understand now . . ."

But what I understand, although I shall not say this to Kira, is the speed at which these dissident artists have come to form an elite caste. Compared with them, the rest of us, the noninitiates, are now becoming peasants, beneath contempt. And yet the author of this *Absurdia* always contrives to eat three square meals a day, while it is the peasants and scum of the earth who provide his sustenance . . . I watch Kira slipping languorously back into the water from her pile of sand, extending her glowing golden limbs full length. "A creative artist . . ." He may, after all, be a good man whose lot I envy. As well as his good fortune in being loved the way Kira loves him.

She lies there, stretched out in our little pool, her eyes closed, her lips on the move once more, framing unspoken words for the man of her life. Despite her beauty she suddenly strikes me as vulnerable. Furthermore, the vehemence with which she criticizes the regime is a sign of weakness: the Soviet society she detests is already moribund. Kira is wasting the best years of her life savaging a corpse. Or perhaps this ferocious stance is the price she has to pay for being accepted in the world of the capital's dissident intelligentsia. She, a poor provincial with no connections, a former pupil at an orphanage. Red Riding Hood . . .

The memory of our childhood returns, the more than sibling solidarity that bonded us together, a redirection onto our schoolfellows of our longing for a close relative to love. The search indeed for an absent mother in the features of a female teacher, a fellow pupil . . . As a child, I must have stared at Kira's face in that way.

I should like to reassure the little girl whose presence I sense deep inside this beautiful, self-confident young woman, in reality so defenseless.

"You're right, Kira. Absolutely right. This society can't last much longer. And your artist friends, I can understand them: censorship, the impossibility of traveling, empty shops. Except that . . . Look at the two of us, for instance. We were brought up in an orphanage, right? Did you ever go without food? No. The same for clothes. It was very simple, but we didn't walk around in rags. And later on you and I were both able to go to college without rich parents paying for private tutors and lodging for us. But above all . . ."

I am interrupted by a mighty shout of laughter. Kira stands up in the pool and hurls great spurts of water at me, with both hands.

"You're a hopeless Leninist! Yes, I remember now. You were the one who dragged us off, me and some other girls, trying to find an old madwoman who'd met Lenin, or so she said! Look, by the age of twelve you were already completely brainwashed . . . It's unbelievable how people still hang on to that rotten concept of communism! You'd be a first-rate propagandist for the Soviet paradise. Free education, free health care. What are you going to give us next? Free rail travel to the gulag, I suppose?"

She weeps tears of laughter and for a short while I begin to have doubts about that vulnerability covered up by her self-assurance. She seems like a young woman completely comfortable in the life she has chosen.

"Go on. Take off your shirt and pants! Do a bit of sunbathing; it'll drive away your gloom. If you haven't got trunks it doesn't matter. We all know Soviet industry only produces a single type of underpants, big enough to fit three fellows like you at once . . ."

Embarrassed and reverting to being a schoolboy confronted by a mocking girl, I take off my shirt, murmuring, "Actually the doctor told me to be careful of the sun. On account of my burns . . ."

My back, in particular, is still marked with red patches where the new skin is delicate and sensitive. Kira abandons her jeering manner.

"Go into the shade. But, you know, those wounds will form scar tissue better out in the air . . ."

Our generation has retained this pious respect for wounded soldiers. Very soon, however, my friend remembers she is dealing with a special kind of soldier, one of those who took part in a war waged by an abominable regime. So this is an army man not entitled to the customary consideration.

"And you still dare to find excuses for those geriatrics in the Kremlin who've turned you into a leopard! Have you seen your back in a mirror? It looks like squashed tomatoes. I hope they gave you a medal for your bravery!"

I hesitate for a moment, then tell myself that, in her eyes, I have nothing left to lose.

"It was even more stupid than you might think. Our helicopter crashed just before landing. When we jumped clear the chopper was already on fire. I was lucky enough to land on something like a mattress—a very big guy. I don't know how many of his ribs I cracked. And this saved me from breaking anything myself. And thanks to me, he escaped burns on his face. In point of fact I took all the heat on my back. We used to tease one another at the hospital. He'd say, 'You smashed my ribs, you bastard!' and I'd say, 'Feast your eyes on this, you swine. This is how your face would look if I hadn't protected you!' And I'd turn and show him my back. Yes, squashed tomatoes, as you say . . . So, you see there was no reason to stick a medal on me . . ."

Kira laughs again, this time with a hint of contempt. And I regret having told her about my regimental comrade. He and I, she thinks, belong in the same category: we are stupid enough not to have totally rejected the world we were born into and grew up in, which is now dying of a pitiful and often ridiculous old age. I ought to spit out this past, deride the people who had the misfortune to live through it, that way I could satisfy Kira and her friends. How can I explain to her that the past of this country, which is on the brink of disappearing forever, also contains our childhood? And this brief fragment of memory, too: high up on a grandstand, in the middle of a huge park covered in snow, I see the pupils from our class, far away, heading toward the orphanage after clearing the pathways, and there, apart from the others, already bridling at discipline, walks a little girl, whom I can recognize by her red hat . . . Must that memory also be rejected? And this apple orchard, too? And its intoxicating beauty? Must it be derided, seen as a failure on the part of a society that promised a dreamlike future and has lamentably run aground? But derided in the name of what other future?

Kira's laughter calms down, she gives a pitying sigh.

"Your problem is that you can't free yourself mentally. You can't even imagine how people could live and think differently. How life could be radically different!"

"Wait, this radically different life interests me. So tomorrow communism's rotten shanty will be razed to the ground. That's clear. But what, in fact, do you and your friends propose to replace it? What kind of society? What way of life?"

"We propose freedom! And a *civilized* society, do you understand? A way of life where you don't have to stand in line for three hours to get hold of a pair of boots. Where you can travel without a visa. Where you can publish your manuscripts freely. Yes, a material and social life to a modern standard. And where you can happily . . ."

"Drive your convertible along Sunset Boulevard . . ."

"You satirize everything. That's another habit of the good little Soviet citizen you've never stopped being . . . Well, why not a convertible? Why despise people who like to own nice things and enjoy life to the full? After all, God created men the way they are . . ."

"Well, I think it was more a case of men creating that kind of god. But let it pass . . . OK, no more satire, I promise. So tomorrow, thanks to your friends, we'll have freedom. Shoes bought without having to stand in line. Thirty television channels. In a word, a multiparty system plus material comfort for everyone, or almost everyone . . . And then what?"

"How do you mean: then what? Well, that's how it'll go on being."

"And that's all? Don't you find the prospect a bit dispiriting?"

The thought that the society her friends long for might become a matter of routine, might lose its dazzle as a future dream, is an idea that puzzles Kira. I suspect she has never foreseen a sequel to the paradise of freedom and abundance that inspires her dissident activity. She stretches out on the sand again, somewhat sulkily, like a child not wanting to admit reality, and grumbles with a sigh, "OK, if you prefer to remain stuck in the communist lunatic asylum, stay right here in this orchard. You couldn't have chosen a place more suited to your tastes. Only, as I warned you, these apple trees are barren. You'll never get a bite to eat here. It's just like the empty stores in this country . . ."

The voice she says it in allows a weary indifference to be heard, a refusal to argue. With a yawn she turns away, stretches out her hand, scoops up a little water, pats her forehead and her neck, then lies still.

I do not reply. I have a dawning perception it is not easy to put into words. I simply sense that in this pointless debate, something essential has eluded us. And this essential point is the red hat belonging to the little girl who wanted to be different at all costs. Her revolt arose out of a violent longing for identity in a world that did all it could to impose a collective, leveled-out life and what it called "social equality." In adolescence she became aware that this equality meant mind-numbing work for starvation wages and cramming several families into one communal apartment. As a young woman, when she wanted to reach for the stratosphere on high heels and bombard the crowd with the staccato of her inimitable footsteps, what she found was dreary queues waiting at counters where cantankerous saleswomen offered ankle boots reminiscent of medieval instruments of torture. She came to loathe this regime, considering that it prohibited her from being unique. All the rest came later: dissidence, drink-fueled secret meetings in kitchens blue with tobacco smoke where, for whole nights at a time, banned artists would read aloud from their unfinished novels, excoriate the Soviet hell, and extol the paradise of the West. There she felt happy, finding in this agitation the opportunity for an incomparable way forward such as she had always dreamed of, yes, the chance to put on her red hat . . .

And then time had gone by and on the threshold of being thirty, a formidable milestone for any young woman, she had come across a former fellow pupil from the orphanage, a bit of an oaf, who could not understand how wonderfully exciting her life was and how mind-blowing the project was that she and her friends were developing for their sorry country. And now, to cap it all, this backward-looking comrade has been stupid enough to ask her a ridiculous question that has nevertheless made her thoughtful. "Imagine your dream has come true," he has said. "The queues disappear, people live in material comfort and travel all over the world the way retired people in rich countries do. But would this collection of benefits totally change the course of your life, give you a happiness unlike any other, the Red Riding Hood hat you used to sport at the orphanage?"

I know what I should say to Kira is just this: "The unique existence you've always been looking for is right here. In this dreamlike apple orchard, like nowhere else on earth. In this fine day poised between spring and summer. In this moment so singular it's not even a part of your life. It's a blip in time, a meeting, a fruitless one for you, with a man you'll never love, me, and the specter of a man you do love. This will never happen again in your life. It's here, your destiny and yours alone. If I were you I'd utter a long shout of joy in salute to the incredible madness of the regime you hate. For it's given you this breathtaking flight through the beauty of this mass of white trees, trees, as if laden with snow, just as they were at that moment when I saw you in childhood, walking apart from the others, with your red hat on your head . . ."

I wake up, realizing I have dreamed those words, utterly true and equally impossible to share with her. Lying beside the water, her head resting on one arm, Kira is drowsing, too, and the expression on her face betrays a childish disarray. In a murmur I now address this sleeping beauty, this little girl of long ago, who shows through as she sleeps. "You're right, Kira, these apple trees will never bear fruit. It's a failed project, like my hope for an ideal city lived in by fraternal men, cured of hatred and greed . . . But just wait and see. Here, in the realm of this barren apple orchard, beside this half-finished fountain, a single apple is going to ripen, just one, an exception to nature's logic, a fruit that'll be here for us, with a flavor no one on earth has ever tasted. We'll have to return in September . . ."

Kira stirs, opens her eyes, shakes her head, gives me a rather defiant look.

A droning noise fills the air, I recognize a helicopter flying low. It was doubtless this thundering clatter, a sound imprinted in every cell of my scalded body, that woke me just now. A little veil of clouds dulls the sun. A swift breeze passes through the tops of the apple trees, causes some petals to flutter down. Kira shivers, I see the reflection of her face shimmering in the mirror of the water, a strangely wan image, that of a bitter woman, weary of believing and being mistaken . . . She dresses and we leave.

At the moment when the central circle is about to be lost to view

behind the avenue's massed branches, I turn: a ray of sunlight picks out
the imprint of our bodies on the sand.

A few years after our expedition to the model apple orchard, the project
cherished by Kira's friends came to fruition. Communism collapsed in
a great tragicomic hurly-burly of palace revolutions, liberal promises,
putsches, appalling economic pillage, edifying credos, and contempt for
the old and weak.

In fact, History overtook this tardy generation of rebels, and the
most exalted of their dreams soon appeared timid beside the savage violence with which Russia was reformed. The nice, cozy bourgeois society
whose advent they hoped for found itself submerged under the muddy
torrent of a capitalism of predators and mafiosi. By then most of the
dissidents had already emigrated to America, where they could meditate
on the unpredictable character of their country, quoting this old adage:
"Russians never achieve their goals, because they always overshoot."

Kira never knew that cataclysmic time. She died in the winter of the year
following our brief encounter. As a rebellious militant, she would doubtless have preferred to perish in a camp or on the scaffold. But it was an
ill-tended pneumonia. I would learn, much later, that she had contracted
it when she went to visit her companion in his exile thirty miles from
Moscow. This version, which I have always tried to believe in, had the
advantage of allowing my childhood friend a heroic life, sacrificed on
the altar of a great cause.

The man Kira was so in love with has been living in Berlin for several
years now. I find his surname, Svistunov ("whistler"), with its comic
hint of frivolity, hard to forget, an uncommon name. His profession, on
the other hand, is not at all rare among the dissident intellectuals of his
generation: he is a journalist, or more precisely a reporter who runs, as it
were, an import-export business in ideas. Sometimes in Moscow, sometimes in Europe, he feeds the Western press with terrifying stories about

the rebirth of dictatorship in Russia and the Russian press with reports on the perfidious designs of the Europeans and Americans . . .

We met recently and he was the one who told me, amid laughter, about this double game. He struck me as a lighthearted, jovial man, barely affected by his former exile. After Kira's account I had pictured a pale martyr with a feverish look, his lips on fire with the truth. As I stared at him I was trying to work out the incredible physical resemblance he had to someone I was familiar with. Suddenly it came to me: Svistunov's smooth, pink visage was not very different from the baby face of "the man who had known Lenin." Yes, that sprightly and youthful apparatchik whose story we had listened to. Only a woman's blind love could have endowed Svistunov's humdrum face with an insurgent's tragic nobility.

I talked to him about Kira. With an emotion that took me by surprise—I had not expected that day spent in the apple orchard to remain such a vivid memory.

"Kira . . . who? Wait, was she a blonde or a brunette? More auburn haired? . . . No. I'm sorry. I don't remember her. Are you sure she was one of my . . . admirers? No. Not even the KGB will make me confess to it, ha, ha, ha!"

He seemed perfectly sincere and it was the one moment when his face took on an air of frankness, being otherwise overlaid with expressions that were always somewhat elusive and ambiguous, as required by his professional duplicity. No, he was not lying; he really did not remember the young woman who had idolized him.

"And your novel, that book you were writing in exile, *Captives in Absurdia*, was it?"

"Oh, that. That was just juvenile rubbish. Besides, after Solzhenitsyn and Shalamov, what is there to tell? They've said it all . . . And, as for girls, well, I was a superstud at the time. And another thing, you know what women are like. They take a great fancy to outlaws, persecuted people, exiles . . . So many came to see me, hordes of them, in that dump in the sticks where they made me live . . ."

He began to tell me about his extremely active and dissolute love life, in total contradiction to the grim picture his generation used to paint of the country crushed beneath the ideology's puritanism. His voice shook with positively nostalgic vibrato. Yes, he missed that youth made up of clandestine meetings, dissident daydreams, and fleeting multiple love affairs, spiced with danger. I saw his eyes cloud over . . . Quickly he pulled himself together.

"So, shall we do it, our little interview? I should tell you straight away, this is for a Russian paper, so . . ."

The fact that Kira was totally forgotten by him upset me at first, as if this ideas merchant's boorishness were directed at me personally. Then I discovered a silver lining in it: for that stroll we took long ago in the middle of the apple orchard's silent paradise had thus remained permanently apart from the lives of other people. My only fear now was of learning that a new freeway had drawn a line forever through that useless orchard's beautiful madness. A motorway, a Coca-Cola bottling plant, or some kind of sports center with swimming pools and casinos, celebratory symbols of the recent upheavals.

One day in a plane flying from Paris to Japan I passed over the region of that giant plantation from the Soviet era. The spring sky was exceptionally clear and on the ground one could see the tiniest dots of houses, the tracery of rivers, the mirrors of lakes. And the line of a road, probably the one linking Moscow and Kiev, which in the old days ran beside innumerable apple trees. At one moment I thought I could see them: a sea of snow-white foam, the vast size of which was surprising, even observed from that altitude. Or was it a long drift of clouds lit up by the sunset?

My fears of seeing that white dream replaced by a superstore were dispelled then. For now I knew that very distant day when I wandered in Kira's company was no longer of this world and therefore ran no risk of being destroyed.

"That apple orchard is still in flower," I told myself. "Time has passed it by, leaving it behind in a moment that does not pass. An idea that seems as insane as the beauty of those flowering trees that will never bear fruit. But to believe in it gives a supreme meaning to our lives, our encounters, our loves."

Then I caught myself mentally addressing Kira, as on so many occasions during these last twenty years.

The truth is, I have never stopped walking beside her along an endless avenue lined with snow-clad boughs.

EIGHT

The Poet Who Helped God to Love

At first I cannot understand what it is about this scene that intrigues me so . . .

The luminous violence of the mistral in these towns, white with sunlight, that look as if they had been drawn on the sails of ships, has left me still dazed. An old friend has arranged to meet me in Nice. Starting the previous day, I have been taking my time, stepping off the train on three or four occasions in places I did not know, as if to get myself used to the idea of meeting someone again after so many years of forgetting. This return to the past was making me somewhat apprehensive . . .

In one of these towns, stunned by this winter wind's sun-drenched ferocity, I had been stumbling as I walked before finding shelter behind the walls of a cemetery. And seeing that haunting female figure beside a grave. The past, whose summons I was trying to hold at bay, suddenly became very present, close enough to touch at the slightest rekindling of memory . . .

My eyes still blinded, I am now watching a strange performance. A heavy, stout woman of about sixty, with a dour expression, emerges from a private room in the restaurant in Nice where I sit at a table with my friend

of thirty years ago. Supported under her elbows by a woman and man
who could be her children, she begins making her way up a staircase. It is
painful to see her contorted legs on high heels, scarcely practical in view
of her corpulence. She has a sullen air and mutters observations between
her teeth, no doubt railing against the stupid idea of installing lavatories
on the second floor. Her escorts concur with comical obsequiousness.

But it is particularly my friend's attitude that strikes me: I sense
that he is uneasy, his gaze travels around the room, settles on a man just
coming in and another, an athletic type with dark hair, suddenly standing up . . .

The stout woman mounts the last few steps of the staircase and,
panting heavily, broadcasts a critique in more ringing tones: in her view
the quality of the cuisine does not match the establishment's reputation.
Suddenly I realize she is speaking in Russian . . .

I turn to my friend.

"Do you know that woman?"

He seems embarrassed, rubs his brow, then comes out with: "Yes . . .
I know her. She's a woman who . . . a woman who, without being aware
of it . . . was loved . . . in a way one cannot be loved . . . other than far
away from this earth."

This friend, Pyotr Glebov, is the former regimental comrade with whom
I once endured the circumstance, both dangerous and funny, of our helicopter crashing and catching fire, our tumbling out, Pyotr's ribs being
smashed by my landing on top of him, my back being struck by a jet of
blazing fuel, thus saving him from burns on the face . . . We laugh now
as we recall these events, as if it were an ancient schoolboy escapade.

What strikes us is the short time it takes to catch up on the more
than two dozen years during which the crucial part of our adult lives has
passed. Sharing the fate of all our generation, bruised by the collapse of
the USSR, Pyotr has tried a thousand trades since then, traveled a lot,
forever seeking to convince himself he was coming to grips with this
modern life, not feeling behind the times.

He describes his current occupation somewhat vaguely: an agent for a firm that arranges for VIPs to travel abroad. His experience of travel must be useful to him and he speaks several languages . . . I do not press him too hard to tell me what precisely his duties are: I can see talking about it embarrasses him.

This reticence was visible from the first moments of our encounter. He did not want to sit down for dinner, preferring just to have a drink. I thought it was a worry over money. "But this is my treat!" He refused again, complained that he had eaten too much at lunchtime . . .

The stout woman, surrounded by her entourage, returns down the stairs. I can study her face better now. The disdainful dourness of an important person's wife, the spoiled manner of one who must be obeyed in all things because she is rich. A heavily powdered mask, features doubtless reshaped by a surgeon, with taut grimaces that lag behind the sentiments expressed. Her corpulent figure is reminiscent of bulges in the bark on tree trunks. And her clothes proclaim their costliness, bombarding the eye with a spangle of jewels. Her whole outfit, excessive and gleaming, is just like . . . Yes, like that luxury car I saw parked opposite the restaurant. I was astonished to see a Russian license plate. I glance out the window: the limousine is still there.

Pyotr has intercepted my look.

"They had it brought from Moscow . . . Instead of hiring a vehicle locally."

"But why?"

"Why are people idiots? Rich, powerful, and idiots . . . ?"

The stout woman has gone back into the private room and Pyotr relaxes. The connection between him and the Russian dinner guests is still a mystery to me. But I am loath to press him for revelations.

"Now, you said that stuck-up old cow had been loved the way no one has the luck to be loved these days, here in this world of ours. A bit like Beatrice by her Dante . . . Looking at her, it's hard to imagine. Maybe at sixteen, young and fresh . . ."

"Even in her forties she was a very attractive woman, I promise you.

And that was her age when the man who loved her died. The romantic novelists' traditional formula would not be wrong in his case. He surely died with her name on his lips. He had never ceased loving her."

"So do you know who this Prince Charming was?"

"You know, too. I introduced him to you once. His name was Dmitri Ress."

I had known Ress too little and too briefly. For a few months before his death . . . The man who had been given the nickname of "Poet" in one of the camps.

His life was turned upside down on account of one poster: the lineup of piglike figures on the grandstand for the parade celebrating the October Revolution, the spitting images of the Party leaders. "Long Live the Great October Pork Harvest!" proclaimed the caption.

Conviction, camp, release, fresh acts of "anti-Soviet propaganda," another conviction, each time a longer sentence in a camp with an even harsher regime. And, two decades later, the outcome of this unequal struggle, a man of forty-four who looked like an eighty-year-old, a toothless grimace, lungs ravaged by cancer, a shaking body that the wind seemed to cut right through . . .

I recall our slow stroll through a big city in a festive mood. The conversation we had, held up on a bridge, as we watched the May Day parade in the distance, lines of people and red flags flooding the city's main square. The devastating coughing fits that overcame Ress, the fiery gaze he directed at the world, the vigor of his words, incredible, given his extreme frailty. And then a brief pause beside a park, Ress turning away as a woman passed by with a child. An attractive woman emerging from an official car, walking beside the park fence, disappearing into an apartment building's entrance. And leaving us with a fleeting trace of bitter perfume . . .

Pyotr Glebov's story finally fills in the gaps in what I knew about Ress's life. The woman who has just gone back into a private room in the restaurant is the boyhood sweetheart, the only love, of that indomitable man.

At the age of twenty-two, intoxicated with illicit literature and revolutionary plans, they launch their bill-posting campaign. Important details: it is the young woman who suggests the subject of the "Great Pork Harvest." At first she is much more militant than he; he is a thoughtful student, immersed in the study of Marx. For, strictly speaking, he is not anti-Soviet. Very soon he senses that all societies produce creatures of the same type: ones that, with zoological predictability, can think only of feeding themselves, reproducing themselves, and yielding to the power of a state that shackles them into mind-destroying tasks, stuns them with substitutes for culture, has them kill one another in wars. Indeed, in his early days, he is more of a freethinker drawn to anarchism. But the poster itself is clearly an attack on the prevailing regime. They put it up at night: a libertarian ecstasy, followed by long hours of love, dreams, pledges. And the memory of those November days will never fade, the fluttering of the first snowflakes, the muted air that smells of wood fires, a heady chill announcing the start of a new life, the promise of a quite different world.

Identifying the culprits is child's play for the police. Traces of paint, a vigilant neighbor . . .

During the interrogation, Ress takes everything on himself. His girlfriend suddenly sobers up, realizing that things are getting serious, bursts into tears, denies all responsibility, lies, sobs, is delirious, begs for pardon. She has highly placed parents, Ress only has his mother, a woman of doubtful reputation, having herself spent time in prison under Stalin . . . The young man gets three years, a merciful sentence intended to give him a chance to return to the straight and narrow. His ladylove settles down. After believing you could play hide-and-seek with the regime, she has just glimpsed the workings of the heavy mechanism of repression. From now on she has only one desire: to forget the errors of her youth, to go back to being a pretty student from a good family, carefree, unoriginal, and, very soon, a happy wife and mother.

In the camp Ress comes to realize how much his surmises as a rebellious youth were justified. He discovers a whole world of ruined lives.

Men crushed day after day by the prison machinery as it turns them into wrecks beyond repair. And the man who managed to cross all the lines of barbed wire one night and was shot down at the last of them. Ress now knows his life will be dedicated to the fight against the bullets that make mincemeat of a prisoner caught in the last line of barbed wire.

The regime does not kill him, for we are no longer in the days of Stalin. With quiet, bureaucratic indolence, it inflicts a slow death on him: trial, conviction, release, fresh trial . . .

Throughout all these years the love Ress carries within him follows the paradoxical logic of those who worship calmly, without hope, free of any mind games. No connection between the former lovers is possible now. The woman is married, in the bosom of a family, she lives on another planet, inaccessible to a prisoner who has just been released and will be back in a camp before long. But dreaming of her is vital to him. If he lost this hope, his struggle would become the mere obstinacy of an embittered man, which is how the judges think of him.

His own existence is of little concern to him: released, he finds work, anything to keep body and soul together, and the rest of the time he reads and writes, accumulating, without a second thought, the incriminating elements for his next conviction. From time to time a woman gives him shelter, hoping to divert him from the course he has set himself. As soon as he senses the danger of such a diversion, he leaves, lives in train stations, in abandoned railroad cars. These "inconveniences," as he calls them, with a smile, seem to him external to what matters. His only aim is to arouse his fellow beings from their numb, piglike composure, to share with them the certainty of a world freed of its flaws, the robust faith with which he is now filled.

He becomes increasingly convinced that his former girlfriend initiated him into this quest for truth. That even in her absence, she still gives him the strength to continue his fight. So they are ever united, as in their youth . . . One of his judges, less insensitive than the rest, refers to this dissident so eager to save humanity as having psychological problems, hoping thus to spare him another spell of hard labor. Ress demands that they name any work by Karl Marx, saying he is ready to summarize the contents in order to demonstrate his perfect sanity. The lawyers are embarrassed. He feels sorry for them: "They're forcing you to declare that anyone who thinks mankind deserves better than a pig's fate is mad."

Tossed from one prison to another, from one haven to the next, Ress at last finds a place of anchorage on his tormented road. During his periods of liberty he comes to the city where his former girlfriend lives and where, twice a year, he is sure to be able to see her go by: on May Day and at the celebration of the October Revolution. He knows that, as the wife of one of the city's leaders, she is present at the parades and immediately afterward goes home to prepare the celebratory meal.

He does not try to speak to her. What matters to him is to watch her go by, close to him, immersed in a life he could have led. What makes him happy, above all, is to feel no regret at the idea of having been exiled from this mild routine of human life.

As time passes, remaining unseen becomes difficult. The violence of his cough gives him away, his gaunt physique and his clothes render him suspect in this residential enclave where the city's dignitaries live. One day, after the May Day parade, his beloved's child notices the odd presence of a vagrant shaken by a coughing fit . . .

That day I was with him on his pilgrimage. Ress turned away, clapping a hand to his mouth. The woman moved on, suspecting nothing.

Six months later it was Pyotr Glebov who helped Ress to keep his rendezvous. It was the October Revolution celebrations . . . The parade had finished, a car set down an attractive woman dressed in a long, pale overcoat, who strolled beside the park railings with a dreamy air, passing two men stationed there in a bizarre vigil beneath a fine autumn drizzle. A tall fellow with broad shoulders and a comically thin old man, who was coughing, doubled up, with his eyes half closed. She moved on, leaving them with a momentary tremor of perfume: followed by her son, she went into the apartment building, where the caretaker eyed the two men reprovingly from the doorstep.

"He died a week later," Pyotr tells me now.

"So that was his very last encounter," I murmur, echoing his words, "with the woman he loved . . ."

Pyotr nods, but with a hesitant air, as if the chronology of this love affair were beyond the simple logic of men. Then he continues his story.

On that last occasion Ress had asked him to take him as far as the river. And on the bank he took off his shapka, drew himself up to his full height, exposing his face to the wind's icy blast. He stood there, motionless, his gaze lost in what lay beyond the waters, with an expression Pyotr had never seen on him before. Hard, proud, victorious. Then a distant smile softened his face, he began breathing deeply . . .

Pyotr turns toward the private room. The stout woman is framed in the doorway, and it looks as if her entourage, which consists of several people, is carrying her, supported under her elbows.

"Oh, excuse me," he stammers. "I have to get going now . . ."

"So soon? But, hold on. What's going on? It's not late, we can stay a bit longer . . ."

"The thing is . . . I work for those people. Guide, interpreter, bodyguard, chauffeur. In a word, I'm their servant. I'm very sorry . . . I'll try to call you tomorrow . . ."

He moves away, slips ahead of the Russian dinner guests, holds the door for them . . . Through the window I can see him opening the limousine doors. In fact a whole convoy departs: this huge luxury car plus two other vehicles, one preceding it, the other bringing up the rear . . .

The room in the restaurant is almost empty, night has fallen, and Pyotr Glebov's story comes back to me as vividly as an experience remembered.

Ress stands facing the cold expanse of the river. The wind sets a fine tuft of white hair on the top of his head dancing. The November squalls are powerful, icy; they strike him in the chest, making him teeter. But he stands his ground, stares at the horizon with his toothless mouth stretched in a painful smile.

For he has won! The regime that has ravaged his life is beginning to show signs of decrepitude, is on the brink of collapse.

Very quickly, however, his hard grimace fades into a detached, almost tender expression. He knows that in this duel with History there can be no victor. Regimes change. What remains unchanged is men's desire to possess, to crush their fellow men, to lapse into the numb indifference of well-fed animals.

He smiles, breathes in deeply, and the breath he inhales is mingled with the river's snowy chill, the smoke from a fire burning in one of the shacks that cling to the shore. And a bitter tang of perfume . . .

"A man who's never been loved . . ." I used to say to myself when thinking about Ress. Even God was no help, for such were the laws of his Creation, based upon hatred, destruction, death. Above all, based upon time, which can transform an adored girl into a stout, heavy woman with a coarsely made-up face, like a pig. No, if God had to confront this world without love, he would be powerless.

And it is this human wraith, this Ress, teetering on the brink of nothingness, yes, he alone who has had the strength to cause the beauty of the woman he loved to live forever.

At the time of our meeting, almost thirty years ago, these were the solemn words I believed were needed to sum up Dmitri Ress's life: a revolt against a world in which hatred is the rule and love a strange anomaly. And the failure of God, whose Creation man is called upon to set to rights . . .

I now remember that at the moment when we left the little street where we had paused, looking out over the river, Ress had confided to me with a rueful smile, "They used to call me 'Poet,' my comrades at the camp. If only it were true! I should know how to speak of the joy and light I find everywhere nowadays. Speak of a moment like this, yes, with the last of the snow falling, the scent of a wood fire, and the lamp that has just been lit in that little gray window over there, do you see it?"

I am convinced now that these words expressed, better than anything, what Ress's life allowed us to perceive. Far beyond all doctrines.

For that day, perhaps without his knowing it, it was the poet in him who spoke.

ANDREÏ MAKINE was born in Siberia in 1957 and has lived in France since 1987. His fourth novel, *Dreams of My Russian Summers (Le testament français)*, won both of France's top literary prizes, the Prix Goncourt and Prix Médicis. His work has been translated into more than forty languages. Makine's most recent novels, *The Life of an Unknown Man, Brief Loves That Live Forever*, and *A Woman Loved* are all available from Graywolf Press.

GEOFFREY STRACHAN was awarded the Scott Moncrieff Prize in 1998 for his translation of *Le testament français*. He has translated all of Andreï Makine's novels for publication in Britain and the United States.

The text of *Brief Loves That Live Forever* is set in Centaur, a typeface originally designed by Bruce Rogers for the Metropolitan Museum of Art in 1914 and modeled on letters cut by the fifteenth-century printer Nicolas Jenson. Book design by Ann Sudmeier. Composition by Bookmobile Design & Digital Publisher Services, Minneapolis, Minnesota. Manufactured by Versa Press on acid-free 30 percent postconsumer wastepaper.